WHISPERING IN THE DARK . . .

Natalie tiptoed out into the main room. The fireplace glowed molten red and she hesitated, accustoming her eyes and trying to figure out which huddled mass was Edan.

That sounds like Joey snoring, she thought, and the mumbler's got to be Simon. There's Faizon, there's Jesse . . . *aha*. There's Edan, in the day bed.

She padded swiftly across the room, leaned over to wake him up and found him watching her.

"Oh," she said, suddenly very aware of the fireplace's heat and the fact that she was above him and he was below her and . . .

"You've got the worst timing," he murmured, smiling.

"Shhh," she whispered, putting a hand over his mouth. "Listen, can I drive home with you tomorrow?"

He caught hold of her hand and keeping it tucked inside his own, settled it on his chest. "Why?"

There's some serious torture going down here, she thought, starting to sweat. "Because I want to talk to you." She pulled free. "So?"

"Okay," he said, nodding.

She blinked, surprised. "Fine. See you tomorrow."

"What'd he say?" Cleo mumbled when Natalie padded back into the bedroom.

"You're driving home with Jesse tomorrow," Natalie said, giving her a smug look and clambering back up into her bunk.

Now she could sleep.

WHEN YOU HAVE GIRL FRIENDS —
YOU HAVE IT ALL!

Follow the trials, triumph, and awesome adventures of five special girls that have become fast friends in spite of — or because of their differences!

Janis Sandifer-Wayne,	a peace-loving, vegetarian veteran of protests and causes.
Stephanie Ling,	the hard-working oldest daughter of a single parent.
Natalie Bell,	Los Angeles refugee and street-smart child of an inter-racial marriage.
Cassandra Taylor,	Natalie's cousin and the sophisticated daughter of an upper-middle class African-American family.
Maria Torres,	a beautiful cheerleader who's the apple of her conservative parent's eye.

They're all juniors at Seven Pines High. And they're doing things their own way — together!

GIRL FRIENDS

#5: DANCING IN THE DARK

Nicole Grey

Z·FAVE
KENSINGTON PUBLISHING CORP.

Z*FAVE BOOKS are published by

Kensington Publishing Corp.
475 Park Avenue South
New York, NY 10016

Z*FAVE, the Z*FAVE logo, and Girl Friends are trademarks
of Kensington Publishing Corp.

First Printing: November, 1993

Printed in the United States of America

To Scott and Scott,
who know about the skunk.

One

The Taylor's front porch light blinked and regretfully, seventeen-year-old Cassandra eased out of Faizon Perry's arms.

"I guess I have to go in now," she murmured, resting her head on his shoulder. She didn't want to leave him but her father's signal had been unmistakable and if she didn't hurry, he'd be standing on the porch in his bathrobe, monitoring their good night kiss.

"Did you have a good New Year's Eve?" Faizon said, stroking her cheek.

"The best," she said, smiling. "I mean, Iron Mike's is fun and all but being with you made it perfect."

"I'm glad." His hands were as slow and gentle as his soft, Mississippi drawl and his dark gaze held hers. "You're so beautiful I hate to let you go." He kissed her and drew back slightly, sighing. "You've been beautiful to me since the first time I saw you."

"Oh, right," she said, blushing and burying her face in his shoulder. "I was almost dead from bulimia. My cheeks were sunken and my glands swollen. I looked like a chipmunk."

"Maybe I like chipmunks," he teased, tickling her. "No, seriously; did you ever look into someone's face and have a sort of sweet pain shoot straight through you and something in your mind whispers, 'That one or no one?' "

"Yes." The first time Cassandra had seen him she'd thought he was an angel and she'd been partially right. Faizon had started as her peer counselor, sitting beside her as she poured out dark, bitter feelings. She'd told him all the things she'd never told anyone else and still he'd stayed, shocked by nothing, understanding everything and then he'd reached through her pain and brought her back into life. He let her know she was allowed to be less than perfect, that her thoughts and feelings, even the ugly ones, were nothing to be ashamed of. He was different from anyone she'd known, his words and his strong, dancer's body were like music—

The porch light blinked like a strobe.

"They're so subtle," Cassandra said, sighing. She'd never had a boyfriend before and was actually surprised that her parents weren't circling the car with flashlights to make sure she was still in one piece.

"You'd better go," Faizon said, resting his chin on the top of her head. "I don't want to make your people hate me."

"They couldn't hate you," she said, stifling her prickling conscience. Well, her mother didn't exactly *hate* him, she just wasn't happy that he lived up in the men's shelter near the highway. And that he was so poor. And that his parents had never been married. And if, God forbid, she ever found out his older brother Nevill was an ex-con, well—

"Cass?" He tilted her face up. "Before, when I said

I wished I had a place of my own so I could hold you all night and you said we could be together sometime in your room—"

"I meant it," she said, holding his gaze. "I want you to be in every part of my life. I mean, when I was in the hospital you only got to see all the ugly parts—"

"Nothing about you is ugly."

"That's sweet but it's not true." She put her finger over his mouth, shushing him. "No, I know what you meant but I want you to know the rest." She stopped, thankful the darkness hid her blush. Her feelings were a tangled mixture of romantic dreams and sweeping, physical sensation that pulsed to life at the thought of Faizon exploring her bedroom. It was the only room in the house where she was free to dance in the mirror-lined studio, to tack-up photos of prima ballerinas and snuggle in bed, planning her future. How would it feel to bring him into her private space?

"I don't want to get you into trouble, Cassandra," he said.

"You won't," she whispered, kissing him. "I promise. Now, are you sure you don't want me to drive you home? I don't like the idea of you walking all the way to the highway in the middle of the night by yourself."

"And I hate the idea of you driving back from the shelter alone," he finished, smiling and opening the passenger door of Cassandra's BMW. "It's not far and besides, this way I know you're home safe. C'mon, I'll walk you to your porch."

Cassandra gathered her things and slid out of the car. She took the hand he offered and they walked slowly toward the steps.

"By the way," he said, pausing in the shadows. "I don't know if I told you but you make that dress beautiful."

"Thank you." And to think she almost didn't wear it because it was pink and she'd been afraid her period, which hadn't shown up since she'd started starving herself, was bound to arrive. Beaming, she smoothed the silky skirt. No period and a wonderful night with Faizon. What better way to start the New Year?

The New Year's Eve celebration at Iron Mike's was drawing to a close. The dance floor vibrated under the confetti-strewn partyers and the air was thick with smoke, beer, and the scent of French fries. The bouncers had broken up several half-hearted fights and up on stage, Corrupting Cleo was beginning to sound slightly ragged.

"Jesse looked at you again," sixteen-year-old Natalie Bell said, dancing closer to Cleo Parrish, the only one of her friends left in the place. The other girls had gone home a while ago and Natalie would've been among them if Cleo hadn't asked her to sleep over. Cleo was seventeen and allowed to hang around until closing because her brother Edan was the lead guitarist in the band.

"What?" Cleo yelled, bending and tucking her long, red hair behind her ear. The neckline of her gauze mini-dress swung wide, revealing the black unitard beneath.

"You-know-who looked at you again?" Natalie yelled in Cleo's ear and frowned when she jerked away. "Sorry. I just figured you'd want to know." Like I'd want to know if Edan decided to honor *me* with a look, she finished in sarcastic silence, glaring at the stage where he was ripping through G 'n R's "You Could Be Mine." She

10

snorted and turned back to her partner, some buff guy in an Ozzy T-shirt. As far as she was concerned, the days when she could have been Edan's were over as of tonight.

I tried to give him what he wanted, she thought, throwing herself into the dance. He didn't want us to be just some casual, physical thing so what did I do? Crawled back on my hands and knees and apologized for treating him like a quick fling. Bared my soul by admitting I was gonna try to like *who* he was, not just *what* he looked like and now, when we decide to start again, what does he do? Promises me he's in it for the long haul . . .

"Liar." She shot Edan a venomous look, then transferred it to the lean, shaggy-haired woman at the corner of the stage. Her skin was tanned bronze and some of it was exposed by the rips in her faded jeans. The single button holding the front of her jacket closed didn't hide much of the bare skin underneath *that,* making the view from the stage a serious treat.

Shiloh. Twenty-something, ex-girlfriend of both Edan and Jesse Torres, the band's lead singer. The woman who, according to Jesse's sister Maria, would put out where and whenever she wanted, with no thoughts of the future or regrets for the past.

So he spends the break with *her* instead of with me like he promised, Natalie thought angrily, dancing circles around her partner. *She* shows up and he leaves me sitting at the table like some stupid second-stringer waiting for a chance to jump into the game. And I don't buy that crap Maria said about Shiloh's father being a big cheese and getting Corrupting Cleo record auditions. Edan and Jesse got with her for more than that.

She swept the clinging hair from her neck and tossed it over her shoulders. Maybe taking it out of braids hadn't

11

been such a hot idea after all. The braids had been way cooler than this huge, moppy head of spiral curls. She was dying of thirst, her crop top clung like a second skin and the waistband beneath the wide, black belt was wringing wet.

"Right?" her partner hollered with a bleary grin.

"Oh, sure," she said, not having the slightest idea what he was talking about. He was pretty blitzed and probably couldn't identify her in a crowd of one but he had stamina, she'd say that much for him. He'd danced with her and Cleo since midnight, when Shiloh had gone up on stage and given the band New Year's kisses. And if that hadn't been humiliating enough, Edan (that Benedict Arnold) had given Shiloh the only smile he'd managed all night and Jesse (that scurvy hound) had given her his apartment key. Cleo had been hurt bad but Natalie, seized by a jealous rage, had found herself someone to get with too, only her payback had gone a little too far.

Kissing Nevill Perry right in front of Edan had been a dumb move. An effective "got-you-back" but a dumb move. She hadn't liked Nevill but he'd been there and he'd been willing, sort of a male version of Shiloh, so she'd used him.

What else was I supposed to do, Natalie wondered, grinding her teeth. Sit and wait until Shiloh was done flirting with Edan and then take him back like I was used to being dissed? Man, if I was back in L. A. I'd just get with the sisters and we'd go kick some butt but here . . . She scowled, measuring Cleo's terrorist potential. Forget it. Cleo was disgustingly robust but it was a soft, mellow type of hardiness, not a threatening one. Cleo couldn't have scared a second-grader into finishing his milk, much less a hardened old crone like Shiloh, who supposedly spent part of the year living with the biker community.

And why should I have to fight over Edan anyway? And who is he to get mad at me for kissing some other guy? she thought, working herself into a serious case of righteous indignation. We're not going out and *I'm* not the one who promised to get with me during the break and then acted like I didn't exist. All I did was give a Happy New Year's kiss to an old homeboy from South Central—

Now who's lyin'? her conscience whispered. *Just because you told Cleo and Maria you ran into an old friend from L. A. doesn't make it true. You never saw Nevill before in your life and you didn't know him for more than two minutes before you—*

Shut up, Natalie told herself sharply. No one has to know that but me. You just back off and let me handle this.

Sure, you've done such a great job so far, her conscience purred.

"Natalie?" Cleo nudged her. "Edan just looked at you." Her wide, amber eyes were troubled. "His aura is roiling around like a big, black thundercloud. I mean, it's majorly freaked."

"What about Jesse?" Natalie said, to distract her. Cleo had the weird ability to see things nobody else did and the last thing she wanted her to figure out was the Nevill-deal. Better to remind her that Jesse, who was a slut if Natalie'd ever seen one, and not the guy she ever would have expected Cleo to fall for, was sticking pretty close to Shiloh himself. "How's his aura?"

"I refuse to look," Cleo said, closing her eyes.

"I don't blame you," Natalie said, glancing at Jesse,

13

who was thrashing across the stage. At least Edan hadn't given Shiloh his apartment key. But maybe that was only because Edan didn't *have* an apartment—

"At least you and Edan will get to talk back at my house tonight," Cleo said, wiping her damp forehead. "I'm beat. You'd think they'd give us a break and play something slow."

"Don't even *think* that," Natalie said, glancing at her spastic dance partner, who shot her a wide, muzzy grin and partied on.

Nineteen-year-old Jesse Torres flung the long, tangled black hair back from his face and frantically searched his memory for the next verse. He had time—Edan Parrish was dealing out a wicked guitar solo—but if he couldn't dig the words out of his ringing head, he had the uneasy feeling this New Year's Eve crowd would dig them out for him.

This should be cake, he thought, closing his eyes against the swarm of flushed, exhilarated faces staring up at him. He should've gone into automatic pilot right around the second set, the lyrics should have risen without effort like the ABCs, but they hadn't. He was struggling for every word, aware of every note and while part of that was distraction over Cleo's dance marathon, the major part was Edan's fault for screwing up the final set's song order.

"We're not playing anything slow," Edan had suddenly announced during the last break. "Cut 'Don't Cry' and 'Hunger Strike' and stick in something else."

"Huh? Like what?" Dusty, the drummer had asked.

"I don't care what, I'm just not gonna play anything slow," Edan had said, folding his arms across his chest.

The band members exchanged puzzled looks.

"C'mon, what is this?" Dusty said, twirling his drumsticks. "We gotta do something slow or nobody's gonna get lucky tonight. You know that."

Edan's jaw tightened.

Jesse looked from his best friend, who, for the last four hours had watched that pain-in-the-butt Natalie celebrating New Year's with every other guy in the place, then over at Dusty. "Hey, it's no big deal. We can change the set."

"We could do 'Move With It,' " Tracer offered.

"No way," Dusty said with an impatient gesture. "Jesse hasn't finished writing lyrics yet. What're we supposed to do for a last verse? Hum?"

That had cracked them up and they'd settled on replacement songs. If anyone had wondered why Edan wasn't hanging with Natalie during the final break, his stony expression kept them from asking. Everything had been cool until Shiloh had strolled backstage, flashing her knowing smile and stroking them all with her dark, whisky voice and even though he felt like a total geek fool, Jesse had pulled her aside and told her some story about his apartment being fumigated for roaches, so no offense but he needed his key back and yeah, he was sorry they weren't gonna get together but maybe the next time she was in Chandler they could do it up right.

She'd taken it better than he'd expected, which was dumb because he should have known she wouldn't have cared. That was her way, that was what made her so easy to know. She'd laughed, making him feel even younger than he was, and digging the key out of her ragged jeans, dropped it into his hand. "Whatever," she'd said and headed for Dusty, who looked like he'd just won the lottery.

Jesse had watched her go, feeling kind of weird. Not sad, because he didn't actually *like* her but sort of regretfully relieved. Shiloh was an all night, hassle-free jam and at any other time, the thought of hanging with her would've been right up there with touring with Metallica but . . . not tonight. Tonight he'd put out for an entire audience, sang and screamed and howled until his throat ached and his eyes burned and all he wanted was a cold beer, a comfortable place to collapse and silence.

Man, I must be getting senile, he thought, squirming. I'd better stick with the fumigation story because if this ever gets out, I'll never hear the end of it.

Except from Edan maybe, who was knee-deep and sinking fast. Jesse glanced over at him, then followed his stormy gaze out into the audience, where Natalie and Cleo were falling all over a couple of drunken yahoos with more muscle than brains. Irritated, he felt like grabbing the mike and yelling, "Hey! Back off!" but didn't. They were Edan's problem, not his. Why should he care if Edan's sister Cleo made such a spectacle of herself, going around in that sheer mini-dress like some New Age go-go dancer and promising that fat-necked jerk she was dancing with a lot more than just a smile?

Edan's solo crashed to an end and Jesse grabbed the mike. He stared out over the crowd until they blurred into one big pulsating mass and the lyrics rose in him like floodwater, boiling out of his mouth and ripping a path through the hot, hazy air.

* * *

16

"Happy New Year everybody," Jesse croaked, raising a fist up over the wild crowd. "Thanks a lot. Good night." He nodded and stepped away from the mike.

"Finally," Natalie mumbled. Her head ached, her ears were ringing, and if she didn't sit down soon, she'd probably fall down but the thought of going back to the Parrish's house with Cleo and finally confronting Edan had her wired. She'd never been in his house before, only in the studio where Corrupting Cleo practiced, and she wondered how close his and Cleo's rooms were. And where they'd have their talk. And what he wore to sleep—

"Later."

"Huh?" She looked up in time to see her partner stumble off in the direction of the door and saying a silent thanks for his ending it so neatly, stood on tiptoe, and peered around the congested dance floor for Cleo.

Cleo was standing at the stage, talking to Edan. His long, tawny-gold hair hung down over his sweaty chest and the veins in his lean, muscled arms stood out like ribbing. His face was cold and shuttered and as Natalie watched from the cover of the crowd, he shrugged and turned away.

Uh, oh, she thought, lifting her chin. I have a feeling this isn't gonna be good.

"Come on," Cleo said, sweeping up. "There's no use hanging around here anymore. Let's go." Wheeling, she cut through the mob then veered off, heading for their table.

"Hey, hold up," Natalie said. "What was that all about?"

"Wait'll we get outside," Cleo said, grabbing her coat from the chair where she'd left it and handing Natalie her black leather jacket. "I have the urge to throw a rock

17

at something and if I don't get out of here, I just may break a bottle over my idiot brother's head."

"Whoa," Natalie said, following her out a side door into the cold, crisp air. The parking lot was jammed with people whooping and blowing their horns and nobody seemed to notice the hunk of concrete Cleo whipped at the rusty, overflowing dumpster or the clang it made upon collision. "So, what's the deal?"

Cleo gave her a pained look. "I'm sorry, Natalie. Edan said he's spending the night at Jesse's apartment."

Natalie opened her mouth, then shut it. Her heart felt like someone was stepping on it. Hard. All this time she'd thought they'd be able to sit and if not actually *talk,* at least find some way to communicate, but now he wasn't even going to be there. "Did you tell him I was sleeping over?"

"Yes," Cleo said, sighing.

"What did he say? What were his exact words?"

"Well . . . he gave me this look and said, 'I'm staying at Jesse's tonight.' " Cleo bit her lip. "And then I said wouldn't he feel kind of stupid being there and he said he'd deal with it, Happy New Year and later for us."

"Why would he feel stupid sleeping at Jesse's?" Natalie asked, then her stomach twisted. "Oh, right. Shiloh." She laughed bitterly. "Hey, maybe they'll both get lucky, huh? Man, this sucks."

Cleo picked up another chunk of concrete and heaved it at the dumpster. It flew wide and bounced soundlessly into the darkness.

"Man, I'm totaled," Jesse said hoarsely, sprawling across the couch. Together, he and Edan had just polished off a six-pack of cola and his aching throat had eased slightly but now his stomach was bloated and gurgling. "Urp. Tonight was really weird, you know? I mean, the air was full of like, static or something. Until . . . urp . . . Shiloh showed up, that is. What's her deal?"

Edan grunted.

Jesse lifted his head and peered through the darkness at his friend, who was slumped in the recliner. "Yeah, I hear you. It was just kind of bizarre seeing her again. Think she's gonna stick around or what?"

Edan shrugged.

Jesse eased back and brushed a strand of hair from his mouth. The darkness was broken only by the faint, glowing streetlight reflecting in through the sliding glass door and the silence broken only by his rumbling stomach. "I gave her my key, you know." He snorted, embarrassed. "Then I took it back. Stupid, huh? I mean, instead of hanging here with you, I could've been getting with her."

"I appreciate it," Edan said, nodding his thanks.

"Hey, I didn't do it for you," Jesse said with a grin. He rolled over, grabbed an empty cola can from the floor and winged it across the room, laughing as Edan deftly caught it. "You think I'd nix satisfaction guaranteed for a bud?"

Edan tossed the can back. "Wouldn't be the first time."

"Nah, this time it's me," Jesse said, scratching his stomach and staring up at the ceiling. "I don't know, man. Everything was a blast until she showed up and then *pow*, Ground Zero. The thought of her on me was like . . . whoa. Made my skin crawl."

19

"Try doing your laundry sometime," Edan said amusedly.

"No, I'm serious," Jesse said, propping himself up on an elbow. "It wasn't even like a decision, it was just like an instinct. Remember when our studio was just an old storehouse and your father said we could use it as long as we cleaned it out? And remember how it was really hot and dry, like mummy-dry, except at one end where the ceiling was leaking and all those termites were eating the beam and we got the larvae stuck in our hair?"

"And ran out screaming, ripped off our shirts and did a St. Vitus dance in front of all my father's customers?" Edan said, chuckling.

"Yeah," Jesse said, shuddering as he recalled picking the stubborn, squirming larvae out of each other's hair like two monkeys. At least we didn't eat them, he thought, swallowing hard. "Well, that's the feeling I got when Shiloh showed up. Just the thought of touching her made me feel like I had a head crawling with termites. Ugh."

"You gave her your key, though," Edan said, glancing at him.

"Habit," Jesse said, itching his tingling scalp. "One I'm definitely kicking. What about you? Would you get with her again?"

Edan was silent a moment and when he spoke his voice was oddly flat. "It's a New Year, Jess. I'm done with the old stuff."

"Good resolution," Jesse said, feeling a twinge of unease. Probably just the soda, he thought, patting his stomach. "Well, I think I'm gonna crash. You want the bed or the couch?"

"When was the last time you changed the sheets?"

"When was my last birthday?" Jesse said, laughing. "The couch."

Natalie lay next to Cleo in the double bed, listening to her breathe and trying to fall asleep. It was a losing battle. Everything, from the fact that she'd never slept in the same bed with anyone before to the strange collection of mystical stones and runes decorating the room to the scratchy tag on the back of the wafty nightgown Cleo had lent her was keeping her awake.

Who could sleep with posters like "Celebrate the Music in Your Soul" or "You Must Embrace Your Past to Understand Your Present" staring you in the eyeball, Natalie wondered grumpily, turning onto her side to avoid seeing the posters tacked to the ceiling. Everything in this whole room has thought-stuff attached to it. There's no eye-candy at all. One good poster of Lenny Kravitz or Slash would take my mind right off stupid Edan and that jerk Shiloh—

"It's okay." Cleo's voice was small and slurred with sleep. "They're sleeping."

A chill trickled down Natalie's spine. "Who's sleeping?" she whispered, half-afraid Cleo was gonna pull an exorcist move on her. She shifted, staring into Cleo's slumbering face.

"Edan, Jesse," she murmured. Her eyes moved rapidly beneath the lids, almost like she was watching a tennis match and her lips twitched into a slight smile.

Natalie shivered. The shadowy room seemed lighter somehow, as if the darkness had shifted shades and the stones on the headboard seemed to be reflecting some kind of soft glow. Oh, boy, I'm in trouble here, Natalie thought, sliding closer to her edge of the bed. The heat under the comforter was making her sweat and the hair on the back of her neck had risen. She opened her mouth, squeaked and tried again. "Who's Shiloh sleeping with, Cleo?"

Cleo frowned slightly and her rapid eye movements increased. Suddenly, her face relaxed. "Not us." Within minutes, she was snoring.

Natalie laid there owl-eyed until sunrise, thinking about vampires and zombies and Stephen King, then drifted into a deep, dreamless sleep.

Two

Seventeen-year-old Stephanie Ling took a deep breath and stretched her arms up above her head. Her back ached from being hunched over the pile of letters all night and her brain felt thick and solid as a brick. The cold morning sun was warring with the softer lamplight and the CD player, programmed to repeat, had played Izzy Stradlin's CD all night long. She had her dead, ex-boyfriend Phillip Fairweather to thank for the CD and player and most importantly, for the new secondhand Ford Escort sitting down in the driveway.

But she had her mother to thank—or curse—for this unrelenting wave of pain pounding against her like high tide.

She blinked, trying to dispel the gritty feeling from her tired eyes and eased back against the headboard. How would you deal with this, Phillip? she wondered, resting her ink-stained hand on the pile of smeared, crumpled letters at her side. What would you do if you found out your mother had been lying to you for the past seven years? What if your father hadn't really abandoned you, what if he'd tried to keep in touch with cards and letters and gifts, only your mother hid them away and never, ever told you?

"Just because she was ashamed he was gay," Stephanie mumbled, closing her eyes. The word sounded alien here in her room, where her father had tucked her into bed and kissed her good night so many times. Gay. Her father. No, it didn't fit. It might be true—according to David Ling's long, lost letters it *was* true—but it still didn't fit. He was her father. How could a father be gay? How could *her* father be gay? How could a man marry a woman, have three children and a house and a life and then decide he was gay and leave?

And how could her mother have hidden away seven years' worth of correspondence just because she was ashamed that her husband had left her for a man?

"Just because he didn't love you as a wife anymore didn't mean he couldn't still love his kids," Stephanie whispered, twisting a strand of her long, straight hair into a knot. "What were we, some kind of package deal? He could have all of us or none of us? Do you really hate him that much, Mom?"

All those years of having an unlisted phone number, all those stony, stubborn silences back when he'd first moved out. All the little, ten-year-old Stephanie's bewildered questions that went unacknowledged and unanswered. One day her father was there and her house was a good, solid home sheltering a family. The next, he was gone and the family was anchorless. How many times had she hidden behind the living room drapes, watching the road until her vision blurred, waiting, praying, hoping against hope that her father's car would come around the corner and pull into the driveway? She'd even known what he would say when he gazed at each of their shining

24

faces. "I missed my girls," he'd say quietly. "Can I come back?"

"Yes," Stephanie whispered, knuckling away the tears. Gay or straight, married or divorced, yes Daddy, you can come back.

"Or I can come to you," she said, wiping her nose on her hand. She'd emptied her tissue box hours ago, cried away all her New Year's Eve make-up, and dripped mascara onto her white ribbed turtleneck. Her heel still smarted from when she'd crashed it down onto Mr. Earl's foot but it had been worth it. The boarder, who'd been living rent free ever since he'd started a relationship with her mother, had sneered when he'd told Stephanie about her father, had called him ugly names and tried to make Stephanie feel the same shame her mother did.

But her shame hadn't come from finding out her father was gay. She'd barely had time to digest that before the most hideous truth had speared her brain. Her mother had told Mr. Earl things she hadn't even told her own daughters and *that* had brought shame and rage and a sense of betrayal so overwhelming that Stephanie had nearly hit her.

"I'll never forgive her for that," Stephanie said, gritting her teeth. "She knew that Daddy still loved us and she let us go on thinking he'd dumped us. *We* couldn't know the truth but Mr. Earl could? Oh, no, there's no forgiveness for that kind—"

A dull, distant thump caught her attention. She slid off the bed and padded to the door. Mr. Earl was supposed to be moving out this morning. Her mother had gathered her tattered dignity and ordered him to leave after he'd spilled his guts last night.

The living room curtains were closed and the split

level's upper landing was shadowy. Stephanie curled her fingers around the cast iron railing, watching as Mr. Earl's bald, gleaming head lurched into sight. He was hauling cardboard cartons into the foyer and piling them near the door. Muttering under his breath, he jerked his futon into sight. His elbow bounced off of the wall and cursing, he kicked one of the cartons.

"That isn't one of our blankets, is it?" Stephanie said coldly as he jerked upright and stared into the gloom, trying to spot her. "I'd hate to have to call the cops on you for stealing, Mr. Earl. Or whatever your name is," she added, folding her arms across her chest. "Tell me, how many other women did you con into letting you live in their houses for free?"

He yanked the blanket from the futon and tossed it into the corner. "There. It was a piece of garbage anyway."

"Hey, it was covering your bed," she said, wanting to wound him for messing up her family. She might not be able to get his money but she'd have her pound of flesh. "Oh, how's your foot? Hope I didn't break any toes." She smirked.

"I should've done you a favor and kicked your butt the first time you got mouthy," he said, clenching his soft, white hands into fists. "Taught you how to talk right to your betters." His educated, accountant's voice had disappeared.

"Careful," Stephanie warned sweetly. "You won't find another woman to live off if you keep on talking like white trash." She stopped, unprepared for the blast of pure, unadulterated hate in his gaze. *I guess I hit a nerve,* she thought.

"Stephanie." Her mother glided up behind her and

placed a cool hand on her shoulder. "Go back to your room. I'll make sure Mr. Earl Cherry leaves."

Stephanie shrugged off her mother's touch. "Make sure he doesn't steal anything," she said, walking away.

"Happy New Year," Janis Sandifer-Wayne called, sweeping into the warm, fragrant kitchen amidst a swarm of animals. Her orange feetie-pajamas sagged at the knees and her bathrobe sash dragged along behind her, driving Isis and Angel, two of the three cats, into frantic, pouncing frenzies. "What's for breakfast?"

"Don't say that word unless you plan on using the can opener," her mother Zoe said, grinning as the dogs romped around Janis, eagerly herding her towards the food cabinet. "Oops, too late. The unspeakable has been spoken."

"Easy, guys," Janis said, tripping over one of the cats. "How come nobody fed them?"

"One of our New Year's resolutions was to stop hogging all the chores for ourselves," her father said solemnly, peering over the top of the Chandler News and pushing his round glasses further up onto his nose. "We thought it only fair to share the fun."

"Right," Janis said, rolling her eyes and reaching through the quivering mob into the cabinet. "You'd think they hadn't eaten in a month. Yes, here. Enjoy." She filled their bowls, struggled out of the middle of the swarm, and grabbing a chipped, ceramic mug, made herself a cup of herbal tea.

"Want some fresh blueberry pancakes?" Zoe asked, flipping her long, blond braid back over her shoulder. She was standing at the stove, spooning batter from a bowl to the griddle, oblivious of the thin, golden stream leaking from the spoon down to her Troll-head slippers.

"Mom," Janis said, pointing to the floor.

"What?" Zoe looked down. "Oh, darn it." She plunked down the bowl and scooted over to the dogs. "Here, Jett."

Jett, the thin, black dog Janis had stolen from a junkie's backyard, lifted her delicate, pointed muzzle and sniffed the air. She followed her nose around to where Zoe stood, then obligingly licked the batter from the fuzzy slippers.

"Better than a vacuum," Zoe said cheerfully, heading back to the stove. "So, did you have a nice time last night, Jan?"

"Where did you go?" her father asked curiously.

"Me and Brian and the gang went to hear Maria's brother Jesse's band, Corrupting Cleo," Janis rattled off, bombarding him with information so he wouldn't ask *exactly* where she'd gone because Iron Mike's was a bar and even though her father was pretty cool, she didn't feel like finding out *how* cool right now. "It was really great, too, because Cassandra isn't bulimic anymore and she's totally in love with her ex-peer counselor Faizon and this contractor-guy named Joey showed up especially to see Stephanie and even though I think she's still kind of sad about Phillip's dying, she was nice to him—"

"She's making all this up, right?" Mr. Sandifer-Wayne said, looking hopefully at his wife.

"Shhh," Zoe said. "Go on."

"Well, Simon Pearlstein was there and he kissed Maria at midnight and she looked totally freaked because they're like, only friends and Cleo Parrish, who's Edan, the lead guitarist's sister, showed up and told us she's transferring from parochial school to Seven Pines this semester—" She stopped to draw a breath.

28

"Wasn't this a TV movie starring Susan Lucci?" her father said, scratching his head.

"Please Trent," Zoe said, scowling. "Don't confuse me."

"And Edan and Natalie had some kind of fight and Simon told Brian I shared my toothbrush with the dogs," she finished, looking indignant. "Can you believe he said that?"

Zoe snickered. "Knowing Simon, yes."

"Maria shut him up good though," Janis said, giggling as she recalled the look on Simon's face. "She told him to remember the serrated knife."

"What serrated knife?" Trent asked.

"The one the girls were going to neuter Maria's exboyfriend Leif with when they found out he'd assaulted her," Zoe said impatiently. "Honestly, where have you been lately?"

His jaw dropped. "Janis, you weren't really going to . . ."

"Oh, don't worry, it was just wishful thinking," Janis said hurriedly. "The girlfriend-abuse grapevine is a much better idea. Not as satisfying," she added under her breath, "but at least it's something."

"And how's that going?" Zoe asked, turning back to the stove. "Have any girls come forward yet?"

"Wait a minute," Mr. Sandifer-Wayne said, holding up a hand. "There are girls in Seven Pines who are being abused by their boyfriends?"

"Well, yeah," Janis said, giving him an odd look. "They're trying to keep it a secret but it's pretty obvious once you start looking for signs. Most of them are still with the guys, too. Isn't that sad?"

"Sad? It's appalling," her father said, falling back in

29

his chair. "Why would a girl let a boy treat her that way?"

"Because they're scared," Janis said. "They're scared of the guy's anger if they try to break up, they're scared of what he'll do to them or even worse, they're afraid that if they lose this guy they'll never get another one and they'll have to be alone."

Mr. Sandifer-Wayne shook his head. "Good heavens, if I had a choice between hanging around someone who hurt me or being alone, it's no contest. I'd stay alone."

"That's because you already know being loved doesn't mean being in pain," Janis said patiently. "These abusive guys find girls who don't believe they deserve any better. Maybe the guy makes a point of showing them every-thing that's supposedly wrong with them and then says stuff like, 'But I love you anyway and no one else would ever put up with you,' which is a major lie, of course, but it's perfect to control the girl with. Or maybe they've watched their mothers get hit and figure hey, if it's good enough for her, it's good enough for me—"

"But that's wrong," her father interrupted, running a hand through his sparse, blond hair. "No man should ever hit a woman, especially not in the name of love. That's not love, that's brutality and I don't care *what* the excuse is."

"And they say chivalry is dead," Zoe said, giving him a teasing smile. "Now where's my rolling pin?"

"Hey, I'm not talking about psycho-attack women from Mars," he said, laughing as she locked her arms around his neck and covered his face in playful kisses.

"Oh, please," Janis groaned, hiding her eyes. "I'm an impressionable child, remember?"

"Good," Zoe said, grabbing her husband's ears and

planting a whopper kiss on his mouth. "There Janis, I hope you're soaking up all this love like a big fat sponge."

"*I* sure am," Trent said with a grin.

"You guys are totally hopeless," Janis said, shaking her head. She was smiling when she said it though, because this kind of happiness only reinforced what she'd come to believe about love. It wasn't cruel or accusing, it didn't hurt you or make you feel small, it made you warm and comfy and it stayed even when you were going bald or wearing Troll-head slippers. Sniffing, she glanced over at the stove. "The pancakes are burning."

Trent jumped up, nearly dumping his wife on the floor and grabbing a spatula, scooped the crusty brown ovals from the griddle. "Whew, I think we caught them in time."

Janis and her mother exchanged grins.

"What?" Trent said, intercepting the silent communication and flushing. "Well, I'm hungry and if we're supposed to be down at Harmony House by noon, we have to finish breakfast, right?"

"Of course," Zoe said, lips twitching. "And pancakes are much more nourishing than kisses."

"Wrong, wise guy," he said, smirking and pointing the spatula at her. "Kisses are more nourishing but pancakes are more *filling.*"

"He has a point," Zoe mused, glancing at Janis.

"Yeah, but we don't have to admit it," Janis said.

"Ha, too late," her father said, high-fiving himself and flinging pancake crumbs into the pack of waiting dogs. "Score one for the old man. What a way to start a new year."

Janis looked from her mother, who was watching her

31

husband with a warm, soft look, to her father, who was clowning around like a mega-geek and wondered why anyone would settle for a love less than this.

"I wish you had gotten home earlier," Mrs. Taylor said the moment Natalie walked in the front door. "You know Grampa and your mother are leaving tomorrow. I would think you'd want to spend some time with them before they go."

And a Happy New Year to you too, Aunt Miriam, Natalie thought sullenly, but didn't say it. One of the first things she'd learned living in Cassandra's parents' house was that it was always better to pretend you were sorry than to go head-to-head with them because they wouldn't tolerate disrespect. "I'm sorry, Aunt Miriam. I had a hard time falling asleep in a strange house and Cleo's alarm didn't go off on time." She smiled and sniffed the air. "Mm, something smells good. Need help in the kitchen?"

"No, we're handling things just fine," her aunt said, not completely mollified. "But your Grampa could use a visit. He's in the den with Carlton and Cassandra." She hesitated, then stepped closer to Natalie and said casually, "So, what do you think of Cassandra's new friend, Faizon?"

Give it up, Aunt Miriam, Natalie thought, stifling a grin. You can't manipulate the master manipulator. "Honestly? I think he's the absolute best first boyfriend she could ever have. He treats her like gold and it seems like he really cares about her." Ha, blew your mind, she thought, enjoying her aunt's irritated frown. Not that she didn't love her aunt and uncle but sometimes they were so concerned about tiny, useless details that they missed the big picture.

"But his background is so . . . so . . ."

Natalie had to laugh. "Man, it's a good thing you don't live in South Central, Aunt Miriam. The guys I hung with back home make Faizon look like a boy scout."

"That's nothing to be proud of," her aunt said, frowning.

Natalie shrugged. "All I'm saying is that Faizon's a good guy." Now his ex-con brother Nevill is another story, she added silently, remembering his sensual drawl and wicked eyes. And his kiss, of course, hadn't been a boy's kiss. It had been a kiss from a man who was trying to scare an underage girl with an attitude. And it worked, she thought grimly. I'll never kiss a stranger in a bar again.

"You do look tired," Aunt Miriam said, cocking her head and examining her niece's face. "Go on in and sit with Grampa for a while. We'll call when dinner's ready."

"Thanks," Natalie said and surprised herself by giving her aunt a quick hug. "Happy New Year."

"Why, to you, too, honey," her aunt said, touched. Her nose wrinkled and she leaned forward, sniffing Natalie's billowing hair. "Whew, you smell like a cigarette factory. Take a quick shower before you sit with Grampa, okay?"

"Fine," Natalie said, surrendering.

Details, always details.

"Well well well, look who's here," Maria mocked, sticking her head out of her bedroom and peering downstairs to where her brother Jesse had just stepped into

33

the foyer and was slipping out of his jacket. "Shiloh's latest disposable guy."

"Huh? What're you babbling about?" Jesse said puzzledly.

"You know what I'm talking about," Maria said, curling her lip. "I saw you give her your key last night."

"Shhh!" He waved frantically, glancing at the family room where Mr. Torres was watching TV. "You know Mommy and Daddy hate her. What're you trying to do to me?"

"The same thing you did to Shiloh," Maria said sweetly.

His jaw dropped. *"Mija!* Don't even talk like that."

"Oh, come off it," she said, sniffing and tossing back her glossy, black hair. "I mean really, how tacky can you guys be, sitting on the stage during break and drooling all over her, giving her your key—"

"Will you shut up already?" He galloped up the stairs and pushed her backwards into her room.

"Why should I?" Maria said pugnaciously. She wanted to know why he'd fallen prey to Shiloh all over again and knew the only way she'd find out was if she made him mad enough to talk without remembering who he was talking to. Jesse, along with her parents, took great pains to keep her pure and innocent until she could be safely married off to some "nice boy." Leif Walters, the "nice boy" who'd tried to rape her the night of the Homecoming dance, had thrown a monkey wrench into her parents' plans but not Jesse's, because no one had ever told *him* about the Leif-fiasco. "If you're ashamed to have people know you go with her, then why even do it? Or are you a slave to your—"

"Es el colmo," he said grimly. *"Qué mosca te pica?"*

34

"Nothing's eating me," Maria said, folding her arms across her chest and matching his glare. "I mean, hey, I guess I should be used to watching my brother and his best friend make jerks out of themselves over some old woman—"

"Mind if I get a word in edgewise?" Jesse said, clapping a hand over her mouth and yelping when she bit him.

"Now I have to go wash my mouth out with soap," Maria said, scowling and pretending to spit. "Who knows what kind of diseases she left crawling all over you."

"I took back my key," Jesse said.

"Probably something nasty . . . what?" Surprised, Maria watched as he plopped down on the vanity chair. "I didn't see you do that."

"So? I did." Shrugging, he gathered his thick, black hair into a ponytail and shook it free. "The only one who stayed over last night was Edan. You can ask him if you don't believe me."

"Like he'd really tell me the truth," Maria scoffed but intrigue had replaced her indignance and she perched on the edge of the bed, eager to know more. Jesse's lifestyle fascinated her, especially since he so rarely gave her the details about things like groupies and what usually went on after the show was over and the lights had gone out. Sometimes he took his protective, older brother role way too seriously. "So, why did you do it?"

"Beats me," he said, leaning back and giving her a wry smile. "The best I can figure, she reminded me of termite larvae and it was definitely a no go from there."

" 'Termite larvae,' " Maria repeated, trying to decide if he was joking but his face was serious and his dark

35

gaze slightly bewildered. It was an odd expression for her brother and she wasn't exactly sure what to say next.

"Weird, huh?" Jesse said, tugging on the ties of his hooded purple shirt. "I lied and told her my apartment was being fumigated for roaches."

"That was a good one," Maria said.

"Nah, she knew it was bull," he said, shaking his head. "Let me tell you, I felt pretty stupid, too."

"You shouldn't have," Maria said earnestly, leaning forward and poking his arm. "That was the best thing you could've done. I mean, why should you feel dumb for saying no to someone who reminds you of termites? I'd never get with someone who reminded me of bugs. Yuck." She shuddered.

"That's because girls are *supposed* to be picky," he said, grinning.

"That's so sexist," Maria said, giving him a look. "Why should a girl be the only one with standards?"

"Because guys need something to live up to," he said, laughing and avoiding her playful slap. "No, seriously. Everybody's got expectations, everybody has an idea of what they want in a person, you know? Some guys want to get with a Sports Illustrated model but will take anything that shows up as long as she puts out—"

"Like you?" Maria asked, raising an eyebrow.

"—and some guys don't care what a girl's personality is like as long as she's hot—"

"Like you?" Maria repeated.

"—and some guys go out with girls who'll do anything they want for the power trip and some guys don't even know what they want in a girl until they find her."

"And *some* guys," Maria said, giving him the evil eye, "want a girl who doesn't give it up the first time out but

36

for some reason, they'll only go out with the girls who do."

Jesse just looked at her.

"You're sabotaging yourself, Jess," Maria said, relishing her brief flash of insight. "You freak because the girls you see put up with all your crap for a one-nighter but instead of looking for somebody who'll make you prove yourself first, you stick to the ones who don't and just keep on cranking about girls with no self-respect."

He blinked.

"So how much self-respect do you have, if you keep on using these girls and letting them use you?" Maria finished brightly, patting herself on the back. "Wow, Simon was right. Human nature really is bizarre. I mean, look at you. You keep telling yourself it's a mutual thing and if they're offering, why not take? But it's way more than that. Why are you afraid to look for what you say you really want?"

Jesse's mouth opened, then closed.

"Hey, I'm not as dumb as I look," Maria said, twinkling at him. "And I'll tell you something else; I don't know what happened with Edan last night but Natalie ran into an old friend from L. A. and gave him a New Year's kiss, which Edan topped by kissing Shiloh in front of the whole world, so if anybody's got the right to be p.o.'d, it's Natalie. You might want to pass that on," she added, patting his shoulder and rising. "C'mon, I smell dinner and if we don't get down there, Mom'll throw a fit."

"Maria," he began, looking even more bewildered than he had when they'd started.

"It's scary to try and figure yourself out, isn't it?" she said, heading for the door. "My friend Simon says he's

37

been doing it for ages and he still doesn't know himself. Cleo's good at this, too." She glanced back, pleased to see his sudden start. "She's transferring to Seven Pines, so we'll be back together again. Isn't that great?"

He mumbled something and Maria, a student of human nature, was wise enough not to ask him to repeat it.

Three

The phone rang while the Sandifer-Waynes were finishing brunch.

"That's for me," Janis said, diving for it and was embarrassed when she realized neither of her parents had stirred. "Aren't you even gonna race me anymore?"

"We know when we're beaten," Zoe said, surrendering her last bit of pancake to Jett, who had lifted a feathery, black paw and was dragging it down her leg.

"Boy, that really hit the spot," Trent said, leaning back and rubbing his stomach. "If that's lover boy on the line, Jan, tell him we said Happy New Year."

"What do you mean, 'if'?" Zoe teased. "Of course it is. After all, he hasn't heard our darling daughter's melodious voice in almost nine hours. It's time for his fix."

"And we get to listen to young love in action," Trent said with a smug smile. "This is better than one of those 900 party lines. Go ahead Jan, answer it. We're ready."

"You guys think you're so funny," Janis said and picked up the receiver. "Hello?"

"Hey, Janis," Brian said cheerfully. "How you doing?"

"Oh, hi," she said, watching as her parents exchanged

satisfied looks. They'd been unashamedly eavesdropping on her and Brian's conversations ever since she'd started seeing him and now seemed a good a time as any to make them pay. "Listen Brian," she said, turning so her parents wouldn't see her grin, "before you say another word, my father says you have a lot of nerve telling everyone I use the dog's toothbrush and the next time he sees you, he's gonna punch you right in the nose."

"Janis!" Her father shot out of his chair. "I never said that!"

"He says you should never have said that, Brian," she said, smirking. "He's freaking out all over the place."

"Wait a minute, I . . . Janis . . . Zoe!" He turned to his wife. "She's *lying*. Janis, you tell him you're lying."

"You'll have to talk louder, Brian," Janis shouted into the receiver. "My father says he doesn't want to hear anymore of your lies."

Her father gaped at her.

"Are you finished?" Brian said dryly.

"Yeah," she admitted. "Actually, all he said was Happy New Year."

"The same to him," Brian said. Then hastily, "No, don't—"

"Hey, Dad," Janis said brightly. "Brian said if you weren't so old he'd beat the crap out of you."

"Noooo," Brian moaned.

Lips twitching, Trent Sandifer-Wayne looked from his smirking daughter to his wife. "And you thought she was going to take care of us in our golden years."

"I guess it's cardboard cartons on the curb for us," Zoe said, licking the last drop of syrup from her fork.

"No, the garbage men don't like hauling away cartons," Janis said, ignoring Brian's background rantings.

"I'll have to teach the dogs how to do some serious digging. Don't worry, you'll end up eco-friendly. You know," she added, pretending to consider it, "the community garden could use fertilizing and I don't see why—"

"That's it," Trent said, turning and nearly tripping over Luna, one of the shepherd/collie mix dogs sprawled at his feet. "I'm going to shower and then we're going down to Harmony House. If you're coming Janis, you'd better get moving."

"Ummm, I'll let you know," she said, weaving her fingers through the phone cord. "Hey, Brian? Brian?"

"You'd better tell him I never said that," he said. "Geez Jan, I hardly even know the guy—"

"Ease down, he knows it wasn't true. Listen." She lowered her voice so her mother, who was filling the sink, couldn't hear her. "What're you doing today?"

"That's what I was gonna say before you blind-sided me," he grumbled.

She bit her lip. By rights she and Jett, the dog she'd recently stolen, should go down to Harmony House to visit the abandoned, HIV-positive kids who lived there but the lure of being able to spend time alone with Brian was a powerful one. They'd been seeing each other for a while but Harmony House, Brian's job, and what seemed like a thousand other commitments left them almost zero time together. What little time they did have was spent hanging in his truck or her Bronco, never in a warm, comfortable place like her house and never for any length of time. And how am I ever supposed to get to know my own boyfriend if we're never alone together, she thought. I mean, I'm down at Harmony House practically every day anyway.

"Well?" Brian prompted. "What're you hatching in your beady little brain?"

"Hold on. Hey Mom, how long are you and Daddy gonna be down at Harmony House?" Janis asked, trying to sound nonchalant.

"You know, that's hard to say," her mother mused. "Could be anywhere from twenty minutes to oh, say maybe four hours. Why?"

"No reason," Janis said, scowling at her quivering back. "Would you mind if I saw Brian today instead of going with you?"

"Of course not," her mother said. "And where was it the two of you were planning on going?"

"Like you don't know," Janis muttered good-naturedly, catching sight of her grin. "So Brian, why don't you come over in like, an hour? The senior citizens will be gone by then and we can let the orgy begin."

"Janis," Brian ground out.

"Believe me, they *know* that's not true," she said, glad he couldn't see her pink cheeks.

Her mother's snort didn't help matters any.

"That was Faizon," Cassandra said dreamily, hanging up the phone and pirouetting across the shiny, kitchen floor into the den. Her voice was soft and her eyes wide and liquid like a doe's. She was still too thin—the bulimia had taken a serious toll—but she moved like a spring breeze.

"No, really?" Natalie said from the floor, where she was helping her little cousin Carlton and her Grampa put together a praying mantis jigsaw puzzle. She was bored out of her skull and the happiness on her cousin's face

42

only increased her crankiness. "Gee, I'm surprised he called. I didn't know they had phones down at the shelter."

"Pay phones," Cassandra said, completely missing her sarcasm. "He says he wishes he could come for dinner but there's a new patient with anorexia at the hospital and he has to get down there and see how he can help."

"Wow, he's really noble, sacrificing his time with you for someone he doesn't even know," Natalie said, arching an eyebrow. "Do you think you'll be able to eat without him?"

"Mmm," Cassandra murmured, going up on her toes. Oblivious to her audience, she extended her leg into a smooth, graceful *arabesque* and held it without the tiniest tremor. "He *is* noble, isn't he? And kind and gentle and sweet—"

"There goes my appetite," Natalie grumbled, cramming a mandible where the praying mantis's eye should have gone and scowling when Carlton removed it.

"And he understands so much," Cassandra said, coming down and doing some weird little turns that Natalie couldn't identify. "I can tell him anything and he helps me figure out *why* I feel the way I do and how I can make it better."

"He's a fine young man," Grampa Bell said, nodding.

"He sounds like a boring young man to me," Natalie muttered.

Cassandra's laugh rang out like a thousand silver bells. "No Natalie, boring is the one thing Faizon isn't."

"Oh, come on, how can someone so good be anything *but* boring?" Natalie said, tossing aside her puzzle piece. "I mean—"

43

"Natalie Bell," her grandfather rumbled, giving her the eye. "What're you doing?"

Natalie closed her mouth and gazed at him.

"You been trying to bring your cousin down since she hung up that phone."

"No I haven't," she said, flushing.

"Girl, girl," he chided, reaching across the table and brushing her chin with one calloused knuckle. "Why you want to make her feel small about loving that boy?"

"Just forget it," she mumbled, feeling stupid and sort of sick. She'd only known her Grampa since Christmas and already he was hollering at her. Well, not *hollering* exactly but scolding and scolding was worse than yelling because it meant she'd done something so wrong she had to be corrected like some dumb kid. "Sorry, Cass." She rose and strode upstairs towards her bedroom.

"Nat?"

"What?" she said, sighing and veering down the hall to the guest room her mother was occupying. She paused in the doorway, watching her mother plop a duffle bag onto the bed, narrowly missing Locust, the stray dog she'd adopted. Elizabeth Bell was leaving tomorrow, going home to L. A. and suddenly, with a fierce rush of homesickness, Natalie didn't want her to. "If Aunt Miriam sees Locust on the bed, she's gonna kill you, you know."

"Then you be my lookout," Elizabeth said, shoving a hank of brown hair from her eyes and grinning. She was sturdy and strong and "built to last," an inside joke she and Natalie had shared once it was apparent Natalie had inherited her body-type. Natalie's father, Peter Bell, who had left right after Natalie was born, was tall and handsome and dignified, a male version of his sister Miriam.

44

His good looks combined with his idealistic dreams of racial harmony had drawn him to Natalie's mother, who was white, but their shared dreams hadn't withstood the harsh reality of everyday life.

"Why do you have to leave?" Natalie said sulkily, pressing her back to the doorframe and sliding down to the plush carpet. "You should stay here. Let the LAPD find somebody else to bust the brothers back home."

"Whoa, we *have* come a long way," her mother said, giving her a startled look. "Don't tell me you're actually gonna miss me?"

"No," Natalie said, then sighed. "Well, maybe. Okay, yeah, but don't let it go to your head. I'm just bummed today." She pulled her knees to her chest and rested her chin on them. "How am I supposed to feel, anyway? I mean, everything is easier when you're here; Aunt Miriam can't get on me for dressing street or missing curfew or whatever."

"Come on Nat, if you live in their house, you have to abide by their rules."

"But they're so into *details,*" Natalie said, frustrated. "How you dress and act is more important than who you are."

"Maybe they believe that's a *part* of who you are."

"But they want everything so *perfect,*" Natalie interrupted. "Don't get me wrong, they're good people and all, but it's always 'no running, no yelling, don't chip your nail polish, do it when I say so, not when you feel like it—'"

"Oh, so they make you toe the line," Elizabeth said.

"They try to make me toe *their* line and I'm not into these details," she said, struggling to find the right words. "I'm like you, I guess. I want to do things, not think about doing them. I don't want to analyze everything, I just want to *do* things. And you know I'm not perfect, I'm not even *interested* in perfect, and there's no way I'll ever be an overachiever and that's great because Chelsea, Cassandra, and Carlton already covered that base."

"Nobody expects you to be perfect."

"That's what you think," Natalie muttered.

"Well, *I* don't expect you to be perfect. What a gruesome idea."

"Tell me about it. I tried telling Aunt Miriam back in the beginning that it was a losing battle but I think she considers me a challenge or something." She shrugged. "Spike Lee has a better chance of becoming the next president than I have of ever becoming perfect."

"Spike Lee," her mother said interestedly. "Vice president?"

"Against the 'Natalie vs. Perfect' ticket?" she said, screwing her face into a reluctant grin. *"Sinead O'Connor* and the odds of them winning would still be better."

"I get the point." Elizabeth unzipped the duffle bag. "So, since you can't be perfect, don't you think you fit in?"

"No, it's more like . . ." She stopped, unable to put her feelings into words. And that's one of the problems, she thought, running a hand through a mass of tangled spiral curls. We didn't *discuss* everything back in L. A. We were too busy just surviving. I'm not used to dissecting serious stuff. I don't even know how to start. "Okay, try this. I already belong because I'm with blood. All I want them to do is let me go my own way. Well, not totally," she said, catching her mother's skeptical look. "I mean, I'm gonna go to school and everything, I just want them to stop asking me what I want to be

46

when I graduate and what I'm gonna do in the future and all."

"Is that such a pain?" Elizabeth asked, grabbing a handful of underwear from the drawer and jamming it into the duffle bag.

"Leave a pair out for tomorrow or you'll have to wear the same ones twice," Natalie said, grinning as her mother whipped a pair of blue cotton panties back out of the bag. "Man, you wear old lady drawers. Why don't you get with the program and do up a thong or something?"

"Don't change the subject, wise guy," Elizabeth said. "Why does it bother you when they ask about your future?"

"Because I'm not done with my *now* yet," Natalie said, surprised because the words fit her frustration. "I mean I'm sixteen, this is supposed to be the best time for me, right? Why do I have to spend it planning what should happen two years from now? Why do I have to think like an adult before I get to be one? I don't care about college, okay? I can barely stand school now; the thought of doing another four years kills me."

"And they don't understand that," her mother said, tossing a bunch of socks into the bag.

"I haven't even told them," she admitted. "Mom, you don't know what it's like when you're not here. *Everything* is planning for the future in this joint. If I fail a test, it's a major catastrophe because I might not get into a good college. If I said I didn't care because I'm not going to college, they'd be on me like flies to change my mind."

"So what *have* you told them?" Elizabeth asked, roll-

47

ing a pair of sweatshirts into a ball and jamming them into the bag.

"Nothing straight out. Just stuff like I don't know what I want to be yet. I mean, did *you* know what you wanted to be when you were sixteen?"

Her mother laughed. "I hate to pull this one on you but things were different when I was growing up."

"Oh, man," Natalie groaned.

"Well, they were," Elizabeth said, shrugging. "But no, I didn't know what I wanted to be. As a matter of fact, I only went to college because my father had his heart set on somebody in our family going and since I was his only kid, I got nominated."

"There's a waste of money," Natalie said.

"True, because I dropped out after I married your father and went into law enforcement."

"And do you regret it?"

Elizabeth stopped packing and gazed unseeingly out the window. "I'm gonna give you both sides of it, Nat. The heart side and the head side. Logically, I sort of regret not taking advantage of all the opportunities that were offered. If I'd have stayed in school and switched my major, I'd probably be brass and making a lot more money right now."

"Who cares about money?" Natalie said, blowing that right off. "You do all right for me and Locust." She patted the floor and the fuzzy dog bounded off the bed and settled under her arm. "You don't hear us complaining."

"A highly unusual situation," Elizabeth said dryly.

"Ha ha," Natalie said, making a face. "So, if you had stayed in school, you'd be making more money and having more headaches because you'd have to suck up to the local politicians and all the rest of that crap. What about the heart side?"

"That's complicated," her mother said, sitting down on the floor next to her. "See, the ideal situation would have been a balance but sometimes emotions drown everything else out."

You got that right, Natalie thought, scratching Locust's knobby head. Every time I see Edan Parrish, my brain abandons ship and I go into emotional overdrive and screw things up.

"The smartest thing to do is wait and figure it out but your heart never wants to wait. I fell in love with your father and helped him through med school. His dreams were my dreams and I don't think I've ever felt so incredibly pure or . . . *invincible* since then. That's what's so great about being young; life is yours to make beautiful." She smiled softly. "So, no, I wouldn't have traded that feeling for all the college in the world. The happiest day of my life was when you were born, you know."

"No," Natalie said, staring at her knees. "I didn't know."

"Because I never told you," Elizabeth said, petting Locust. "It was mushy stuff and you were always too busy running around like a wild thing to be mushy."

Natalie gave a small laugh. "I still am."

"And that's what worries me," her mother said, laying a strong, square hand on Natalie's arm. "If I'd made more money, you wouldn't have had to grow up on the streets of South Central. You could have grown up in a place like this, with grass and mountains and woods and no drive-bys or gang wars."

"But I liked the 'hood," Natalie protested. "Well, until it almost killed me. I learned a lot there."

49

"But you lost a lot, too," Elizabeth said. "You saw things that made you grow up faster than you should have had to. Well, physically at least."

Natalie's eyebrows rose. "What, you don't think I'm grown-up mentally?"

Elizabeth gave her a long, searching look. "I heard what happened with you and Cassandra and Grampa before, Nat."

Natalie flushed and examined the inside of one of Locust's shaggy ears. The dog shot her an affronted look and tried to pull away but Natalie held firm because the only other place to look was into her mother's face. "Well, Cassandra was being gross, acting all starry-eyed and stuff. You didn't see her—"

"I didn't have to. She's in love."

"Oh man, not you too."

"Natalie," Elizabeth said softly, "don't ruin her happiness just because you don't believe it's ever gonna happen to you."

Natalie's head shot up. "I didn't!"

Her mother looked at her.

"Quit that," Natalie snapped, glancing away. "See, you don't get it either. Cassandra's like, so innocent. She's never got with a guy before for *anything*. I just don't want her to go trusting Faizon with all of herself and then have her get hurt. Man." She rose and shook her head. "Why does everybody think I'm only being real with her because I'm jealous?"

"I don't know," her mother said, leaning back on her hands and meeting her daughter's belligerent gaze. "Why?"

"Forget it," Natalie said and stomped off to her room.

* * *

"Come on in, Brian," Janis shouted, body-blocking three hysterical dogs and a trio of curious cats from the front door. "Hurry, I can't hold them back much longer," she added, grabbing Luna and Topaz's golden-brown ruffs and trying to assert some alpha-dog authority. "No!"

The door opened a crack. "Where's that maniac Jett?" Brian asked, peering in with one suspicious, brown eyeball.

Jett, recognizing her name and Brian's voice, let out a series of eager, high-pitched barks that even overrode the Janis Joplin album blasting away on the turntable.

"Will you come in already so she can bite you and get it over with?" Janis called exasperatedly, throwing her arms around the dog's neck and dragging her from the door.

"The last time she grabbed me she almost pulled all my hair out," he said, his one eye glaring at the salivating dog. "Why don't you lock her up or something?"

Janis's jaw dropped. " 'Lock her up?' This is her *home,* you don't lock people up in their own home—"

"She's not 'people,' she's a dog," he said, transferring his marblelike gaze to her.

"Hmph, that shows how much you know. Now, will you get in here before the rest of the neighborhood thinks you're a burglar and comes after you with pitchforks?"

"Geez, really?" His eye disappeared for a moment. "I thought you guys were all nonviolent."

"Brian, please," she ground out, grabbing Isis. "Now stop it. You know better than that."

The cat jerked her tail and stalked away.

"Okay, here I come," he said, slipping quickly inside. The next few moments were pure chaos.

"It's okay, really," Janis said, patting Brian's rigid shoulder as he flattened his back against the door. "Dogs always sniff each other for identification purposes. It's only natural they should sniff you, too." She glanced down at the furry trio, who seemed determined to store Brian's scent to their collective memories forever and decided she didn't like the gleam in Jett's eyes. The last time Jett had looked so wicked she'd grabbed a mouthful of Brian's hair and played a vigorous game of tug o' war.

"What're you laughing about?" Brian said worriedly.

"Nothing," she said, deciding he wouldn't see the humor in it. "Okay, guys, that's enough. Go find somebody else to harass." She stepped in between the dogs and Brian and gave him a quick kiss. "Mmm, you smell good. Like crisp celery or the ocean. Come sit down. Want something to drink?"

"Uh, okay. What've you got?" he said, following as she waded through stacks of books, newspapers and general clutter toward the couch.

"Grape juice made from migrant worker friendly vineyards or grape yards or whatever they're called," she said, shoving aside a pile of old albums and motioning him to sit. "Apple juice, same deal, veggie juice, water, herbal tea. I can see what kind of herbals we have but I know for sure we've got blackberry, chamomile and—"

"How about a soda?" he said hopefully.

"No go," she said, giving him an amused look. "My parents would rather stock the pantry with deadly nightshade than bring soda into the house."

"I was afraid of that," he muttered, running a hand over his thick, chestnut hair and shooting Jett, who was perched at his knee, a wary glance. "Why does this dog hate me so much?"

"She doesn't hate you, she holds you in the highest esteem," Janis said, plopping down next to him and patting the cushion. Jett scrambled up, followed by Luna and Topaz, who was forced to settle on Brian's side. "She considers you her official pack playmate. She only bites in fun."

"That's what Hannibal Lecter said, too."

Janis laughed and rested her head on his shoulder. "I'm glad we're spending today together, just you and me."

He grunted, craning his neck to keep an eye on the three large cats slinking towards the couch. "How many animals do you have, anyway?"

"Just six," she said, snuggling against him. "Oh, and Star, the skunk we rescued from that vile steel-jaw trap, but she's sort of dormant right now. I could take you out to meet her but she's under the back porch and we'd have to crawl through the mud—"

"No, that's okay," he said, sliding his arm around Janis. "Six is enough for me."

"Really? I wish we had more," she said, smiling as Serene, Angel, and Isis leaped up and padded along the back of the couch. Angel sniffed the base of Brian's neck, sneezed and narrowing her eyes, started digging.

"Hey!" He shot forward, dislodging Topaz, who'd had her head resting along his knee. "That cat's growling!"

"She's *purring,*" Janis said, giggling. "She likes you. Just lean back. I guarantee she'll start kneading your neck like it's her mother's belly and go to sleep."

"But I don't *want* to be her mother's belly," he said, shooting the cat a dark look and hunching his shoulders up around his neck. "It gives me the creeps. And besides, how do I know she won't bite me like that one does?"

He jerked a thumb at Jett, who yawned and rolled onto her back, stretching her head across Janis's lap to his. "Oh man, this place is bizarre."

"Do you really think so?" Janis asked, curious. She'd lived this way all her life and it didn't seem bizarre. It seemed warm and cozy and everything she wanted her own house to be someday. Sure, the wallpaper was faded and the hardwood floors were scuffed and scratched but the furniture had been worn into body-cradling curves and the scent of blueberry pancakes and home-baked bread still hung in the air. She gazed at her beloved animals, at the family photos clustered on the walls, the books, magazines, albums and pet toys covering every flat surface, the Janis Joplin tunes wailing from the turn table and said, "What's so bizarre about it?"

Brian shot her a disbelieving look. "Are you serious?"

"Yeah," she said, withdrawing slightly so she could watch him. "Tell me, because I really don't know."

He cleared his throat, looking like he wished he'd never even brought it up. "Uh, I don't think—"

"C'mon Brian, you won't hurt my feelings. Unless you insult me, of course," she said, making a point of tapping her fingers against Jett's gleaming, white fangs.

He shifted uneasily. "Well, it's not like everybody lets their animals sit on the furniture."

"Really?" Her eyebrows rose. "Where do they sit, then?"

"On the floor, where they belong."

"Oh, you mean *those* kind of people," she said with a sniff. "They're the ones who perpetuate the human animal versus non-human animal prejudice that's so rampant in this country."

"Huh?"

She wiggled around to face him. "Look, when someone judges the value of love by how hairy the one who loves them is, that's like saying Jett's love isn't as valuable because she's a dog, which in turn cheapens my love for her, see? Those people place more importance on possessions than what *really* counts. Why should it matter where love comes from, as long as it's there?"

"I'm not saying love doesn't matter—" he began.

"You're saying it's worth less than furniture, though," Janis said, clambering up on her knees and reaching behind the couch, plucked a wooden plaque from the table. "Listen to this, Brian. Chief Seattle of the Dwamish and allied tribes of Puget Sound said it." She brushed the hair from her face and looking earnest, read, *'What is man without the beasts? If all the beasts were gone, men would die from great loneliness of spirit, for whatever happens to the beasts also happens to the man.'* " She gazed at him, eyes shining. "Isn't that beautiful?"

"I guess," he said. "Though it's kind of far out."

"No, it's not," she said, replacing the plaque. "It makes perfect sense. I would die of loneliness without my non-human sisters. A diamond can't keep you company and you can't snuggle up to a bank account. Possessions don't feed your spirit. I feel sorry for people like that."

"Like what?" he asked, frowning.

"The ones who base their self-worth on how many people they can impress," she said quietly. "They got lost somewhere along the way, because when your couch is so important that your loved ones aren't allowed to sit on it, you've got a serious problem."

"What if people just can't stand getting everything covered with dog hair?" he asked, glancing ruefully at his own pants.

"Whenever you share your life with someone, they're gonna leave evidence of their existence," Janis said, scraping a small, golden fuzzball from the knee of Brian's jeans. "People put up with all kinds of crap from their own species but they freak over a little dog hair. Weird."

"I guess I never thought of it that way," he said, glancing down at her and smiling. "Not that I think you're *totally* right."

"You don't have to think I'm totally right, as long as you can open your mind to my way," she said, tilting her head back and accepting his kiss. "Now, what else is bizarre around here?"

"Forget it," he said huskily, kissing her again.

"But I don't want to forget it," she said, grinning. "This is the first time you've been to my house and I've *never* been to your house, so it's a good education for me. It'll give me an idea of what to expect from your place. So, babble on."

"Okay, let me ask you this; are you guys spring cleaning or something?" he asked, looking around the cluttered room. "I mean, why is all this stuff laying around?"

"What stuff?"

"Oh, c'mon Janis, all these books—"

"Well, we're reading most of them," she said puzzledly. "My father keeps his next to his chair and me and my mother keep ours where we can get to them easy. All the bookcases are already filled. Why? Where do you keep your books?"

"We don't have any books. I mean, my mother has like, fashion magazines and my father has his trade publications—"

"Ah, yes, my favorite, the fur trade," Janis said, giving

him the evil eye. "So you're saying that the only thing a person can learn about in your house is clothes and how to skin dead animals?"

"Geez, don't put it like that," he said, squirming slightly. "You make me sound really stupid."

"No," Janis said. "There's a big difference between being stupid and being ignorant. Stupid is like, lacking intelligence. Ignorant is lacking information, like being uninformed. *Everyone* is ignorant of something. I'm ignorant of all kinds of stuff but every time I read, I find out a little more. So, we're both ignorant."

"I'm not too sure how I feel about this," Brian muttered.

"Well, look at it this way," she said cheerfully. "Now you know that when you come to my house you're gonna be surrounded by animals and there's no soda and my cat thinks the back of your neck is her mother's belly. And now I know that when I go to your house, I should expect no animals . . . well, no *living* animals, lots of Coke, a fashionable mother, and no books."

"You forgot the two most important things," he said with a good-natured smile. "I'll be there and you'll be there."

"Oh, yeah," she murmured, leaning into him. The kiss started gently and grew in intensity, drawing them together and easing them down across the couch. The animals leaped to the ground with a series of soft thuds and the album warbled to an end. Silence blanketed the room like thick, rich velvet. Time drifted, there was only his mouth against hers, the sweep of his warm breath on her cheek and the deep, steady rhythm of her heart.

"Crap," Brian muttered, withdrawing slightly.

"Huh?" Janis said dazedly, yanked back into the Land of the Living. "What's the matter?"

"Look." His voice was a mixture of laughter and frustration. "We have an audience."

She lifted her head and found six animals sitting patiently on their haunches in front of the couch, following their every move. "Oh, no," she said, starting to laugh.

Jett lifted a feathery paw and raked it across Brian's arm.

"I don't suppose she just wants to shake," he said.

"No, that's her please, I have to go out, paw," Janis said, sighing.

"And I don't suppose you just open the door and let her go," he said resignedly.

"No, they all have to be leashed and walked around the yard," Janis said, sitting up and smoothing her hair. Her purple, skinny-rib top had inched up out of her jeans and her lips felt soft and bruised. Like an overripe plum, she mused, glancing at Brian's mouth. Correction; *two* overripe plums. Now I know how parents can tell when their kids have been messing around.

"Next time we're going to my house," Brian warned but his eyes were twinkling and the kiss he gave her held a promise.

Four

"Hey, Steph? Are you gonna have lunch?" Ten-year-old Corinne Ling called curiously, knocking on Stephanie's bedroom door. "Mom said not to bother you but I'm making sandwiches and I need to know whether you want salami or bologna."

"Thanks anyway, Cor, but don't worry about me," Stephanie said, wiping her eyes on her sleeve. She'd re-read her father's letters, had traced his tone from apologetic to bewildered to sorrowful to resigned. She'd counted up seven years' worth of birthday and Christmas presents and the pile of cash next to her totaled over fifteen-hundred dollars. She, his oldest, first-born daughter had never answered even one of his letters and he had still come through for her.

"Well, I won't let Ana hog all the salami so they'll be some left for you later," Corinne said, scampering off down the hall.

And if he came through for me, then he came through for Ana and Corinne too, she thought numbly. All those birthdays when we were too poor to even buy cards could have been avoided if my mother had just given us our mail! She didn't even have to tell us he left because he was gay if it bothered her so much . . .

Stephanie leaned back, trying to focus on that but it kept slipping away. It was almost like her mind had put up a wall to keep her from dealing with it.

"My father is gay," she whispered, then shook her head. No he wasn't, he was her *father*. Yes, he was gay because he'd left her mother for another man. A man he loved more than he'd loved them. "No, that's not true," she said quickly. People divorced everyday, it didn't mean they loved their kids any less. But then how could they just leave? How could they abandon the kids they'd created, just to start a new life? What about all the people they left behind? Didn't *their* feelings count for anything?

"I'm beginning to understand how you felt, Phillip," she said, brushing a hand across her damp eyes. "Your parents made you and they didn't even go through a rotten divorce, they just went back to their own lives and left you. My father made a choice to leave and my mother made a choice not to tell me why. So what's the difference between your parents and mine? All four of them are doing what *they* want to do whether or not it's good for us. We're just this by-product that either goes along with it or . . . what? Dies?"

She ran across the room to the CD collection Phillip had left her and slapped Metallica's "The Unforgiven" onto the player. She needed something dark right now, something to court the anger smothering her heart.

"It's a betrayal," she said. "Parents are not supposed to betray their kids because we *trust* them. They're all we have, they're the only ones who are supposed to be there for us *no matter what*. So what happens instead?

60

They change their minds and we're left to dig up some-body somewhere who cares. Oh, Phillip, you knew this from fourth grade on just like I did, didn't you? No won-der we found each other. No wonder we never cheated on each other; we'd been cheated way too much already."

Corinne's laughter echoed down the hall, followed by Anastasia's scornful, thirteen-year-old drawl.

They were there in the kitchen, the balance of her fam-ily.

"Help me, Phillip," she said, gazing at the photos on the bureau. "How am I supposed to deal with this? My parents might stink but they're the only ones I have and I don't know if I should give up on them yet. I used to love my father, so can't I still love him or am I making it too simple? I mean, if he and my mother had divorced over another woman, I'd resent the other woman for breaking up our house, so isn't it normal that I'd resent his leaving for *any* reason? And that I'd want to punch my mother for never even telling me where he'd gone or realizing that all my nightmares were because one day I had no father?"

She stared at her hollow-eyed reflection in the mirror, wondering when she'd decided the being gay part wasn't the most hurtful issue here. She *still* couldn't imagine him with another man, even though his most recent letter had contained photos of him and his live-in, Ron, a tanned man with curly black hair and a pair of startlingly blue eyes. They'd been standing in front of a trolley car, half-smiling, half-squinting into the camera and although her father looked older, he also looked very happy.

She took a deep, shaky breath and rubbing her frigid hands together for warmth, opened the door. "Mom?

Could you come here, please? I want to talk to you for a minute."

Jesse Torres left his parents' after dinner and whipped his red 300Z out to the Parrish's house. Edan's van, Cleo's Jeep, and the flower farm delivery trucks were in the driveway and he angled around them, parking near the stone studio and sliding out into the chill wind. He could have gone into the farmhouse—Mrs. Parrish would have added another plate to the table as easily as if he belonged there—but for some reason, he wasn't in the mood to deal with family, anybody's family, right now. His sister's question stuck to him like a burr and no matter what else he tried thinking about, it kept scratching his brain, waiting to be answered.

"Well, it can wait forever for all I care," he muttered, flicking on the studio lights and closing the door behind him. "I'm gonna finish writing the lyrics to 'Move With It,' then I'm gonna sing it and Edan's gonna play it out, okay? Okay."

He dropped his jacket onto one of the rickety chairs and headed across the room to the couch against the wall. The old, faded sofa had seen some action, the least being writing songs.

"Man, I don't think I ever sat here alone before," he said, grinning to himself and grabbing a pad and pen from the coffee table, settled back against the lumpy cushions. "Now, where'd I leave off?" He shuffled through the pages, shaking his head at Dusty's lewd, caveman stick-people drawings and was glad he'd never let his sister go out with the Dust-man, no matter how much Dusty had bugged him. "I would've had to kill him and then we'd be out a drummer."

He found the page with the scrawled lyrics and read them. Then reread them. "These suck," he said, frowning and tucking his long, black hair behind his ear. " 'Let's move with it, before the darkness dies, before you burn my eyes?' " He laughed, more embarrassed than amused. "The refrain's okay but the rest is like, whoa." He gnawed the end of the pen. "Maybe it should be a ballad. Yeah, but Corrupting Cleo isn't really a ballad band—"

The door banged open and Cleo Parrish, red hair flying in the wind, swept in. "Hi," she said breathlessly, bumping the door shut with her butt.

"Hey, what's up?" he said, turning the pad over so she wouldn't see his wretched attempts at songwriting, and rising.

"Here," she said, laying a foil-covered dish on the table. "Happy New Year. My mother sent you out a turkey sandwich with stuffing and four brownies for dessert. Enjoy." She smiled briefly and turned to leave.

"Where are you going?"

"I don't want to bother you."

"You're not bothering me," he said, peeling up the foil and gazing at the thick, mayo-smeared sandwich. He loved turkey and it smelled almost too fresh to pass up but if he ate it now he'd probably get mayonnaise all over his face and turkey stuck between his teeth. Sighing, he covered it back up. "I'll wait a while. I'm still kind of full from my own lunch."

"Are you sure?" she said, eyes twinkling.

"Yeah. Why don't you take off your . . . uh . . ." He eyed her brown, hooded cloak uncertainly, wondering what to call it and then surrendered to impulse. "Why

63

don't you park your broom, take off your cape, and hang out for a while?"

"Charming, Jess," she said, laughing and shedding the voluminous cape. Underneath she had on a red gauze mini-dress, a brown unitard and a pewter amulet hung around her neck.

"Don't you ever get cold wearing stuff like that?" he asked, gazing at the thin, nearly-sheer material and wishing she'd left the cape on. There was something very distracting about looking right *through* someone's clothes.

"I have extremely warm blood," she said solemnly, holding out a hand. "Here, feel."

"That's okay, I believe you," he said, ignoring her outstretched hand because his own felt oddly damp. He jammed it into his jeans' pocket, hoping the gesture looked casual. "So where's your brother? Edan, I mean?"

"It's okay, I know his name," she said, turning and weaving through the tables towards the stage. "He's finishing lunch. He should be out soon. As long as I'm here I might as well start taking down the Christmas decorations."

He glanced up at the shriveled mistletoe suspended over the door. As far as he knew, nobody had used it. I must be losing it, he thought, shaking his head. First, I'm alone on the couch, now I'm alone under the mistletoe—

"Isn't that amazing?"

"Huh?" He jerked his gaze from the mistletoe to Cleo.

"I said, I can't believe vacation went so fast."

"Oh, yeah, right. Now back to the grind. Maria says you're starting at Seven Pines soon," he said, ambling towards the stage. She was crabbing along the floor, pry-ing the thumbtacks from the dry, crispy pine garland she'd strung up earlier. "Here, let me get the tacks. You'll break your fingernails."

"Too late," she said carelessly. "My hands are functional Jess, not decorative. I'll pry the tacks, you can hold them. Here." She plopped the first one into his palm. "Yeah, me and Father Dusal came to the conclusion that I wasn't exactly cut out for parochial school."

"But they knew you weren't Catholic when you started, so what's the big deal now?" he said, staring down at the top of her head and expecting to see darker roots sprouting from her scalp. There were none. They were all the same shimmery, reddish-gold but he still found it hard to believe that hair once so screamingly red had mellowed into such a pleasing color. Pleasing? he thought, catching the direction his mind had taken. No way. Try less horrible.

She gave him a weighty look. "Let's just say my spiritual beliefs had never been an issue before this year."

"Hold on," he said as a nasty suspicion wormed its way into his mind. "Don't tell me you started in with all that nutty aura and mysticism stuff—"

"Jesse," she said, sitting back on her heels. "My spiritual beliefs are my own, just like yours are your own. That's the whole concept behind religious freedom, okay? Now, we can discuss our differences if you want but if you attack my beliefs I'm going to have to defend myself and I may end up attacking *yours*, which nobody has the right to do to another person. Now, why don't you just drop it?"

"Okay," he said, staring at her. Her voice was low and rich, full of strength and tinged with an unmistakable warning.

"Excellent," she said, smiling and plopping another tack into his hand. "So, did you find any surprises under the Christmas tree this year?"

He scrambled to switch mental gears. "Oh, yeah, that rock. Thanks," he said, not believing how stupid he sounded. *That rock.* Duh. *That rock* had found a permanent home in his pocket along with his keys and his wallet. "What's it called again?"

"A Tiger's Eye," she said amusedly.

"Yeah," he said, nodding as the rest of her message came rushing back. "You said it's used to separate false desires from what's really needed, right?"

"Good memory," she said. "So, how's it doing?"

He shrugged. What was he supposed to say, that anybody who believed a rock could influence your mind was in big trouble? If he said that, she'd probably come right back at him with some kind of annoying comment about his realizing he hadn't really wanted Shiloh, so he'd blown her off . . .

"Well?" she said with a small, knowing smile.

"That wasn't because of the stone," he blurted, before he realized she couldn't possibly know what he was referring to.

"Maybe," Cleo said serenely, removing the last tack and gathering the stiff, flaking garland into her arms. "But you did it, all the same."

A shiver snaked down his spine. "Did what?" he said, trying to look like he wasn't completely freaked. She knows, he thought, swallowing hard. I don't know how she knows but she knows. And then, Oh God, if she knows about that, what the hell else does she know?

She rose and cocking her head, gave him a twinkling

66

look. "I could tell you but your aura's already sort of a pea greenish. Are you sure you want to know?"

He stared at her, wondering dimly why the room was so hot. His hair felt like it was plastered to his neck and the small of his back was puddled with sweat. "You," he croaked, pointing into her face, "are a mental case." Oh, great Jess, he thought, closing his eyes. Confront a nut, quote Jackie Gleason.

Cleo laughed and patted his arm, making his skin tingle. "Don't worry, I won't hold it against you," she said and trailing pine boughs, picked up her cloak and walked out.

"Whoa," he said, dropping the handful of tacks and leaning back against the stage. His heart was pounding but his neck was cool and dry and the heat in the room had faded. "She's either a great liar or a serious psycho and either way it's all your fault, man. You were the one who ragged on her for not skiing down that slope three years ago. You were the reason she hit that tree and died." He rubbed his forehead, feeling sick. "Jesus, you messed her up big time. No wonder she hates your guts. I'd hate you too if you screwed me up like that."

He paused, then shook it off.

He could have sworn he'd heard someone laughing.

"Sit down please," Stephanie said as her mother came into the room. She didn't want to touch her, could barely stand to look at her and knew if she couldn't keep this discussion on a formal level, she'd end up screaming.

Mrs. Ling perched on the edge of Stephanie's bed and knitted her fingers together in her lap. They twitched slightly but all the light, fluttery movements had been stilled.

The sparrows have died, Stephanie thought, hating the sudden ache in her throat. Oh, Mom, why did you have to be so afraid?

"Mr. Earl Cherry has left us," Mrs. Ling said, staring down at her hands. "The room is vacant again. We'll have to advertise for another boarder."

"A woman this time," Stephanie said and the darkest part of her was glad to see her mother wince.

"Yes," Mrs. Ling agreed quietly. "A bitter, friendless woman so she and I can keep each other company. A woman who has been shamed not only by her husband but by her children—"

"I didn't shame you, Mom," Stephanie said, ignoring the stab of pain piercing her chest. "You shamed yourself with Mr. Earl. All I did was point out what you couldn't see."

"I saw," Mrs. Ling said, lifting her head and meeting her daughter's angry gaze. "And I accepted what was offered, which was my right."

"What about *our* rights? We live here too, you know."

"And you would have benefited from knowing Mr. Earl, if you had given him a chance," Mrs. Ling said, ignoring her daughter's scornful snort. "But you judged him without taking into account our situation. What man would want a shamed, divorced woman with three girls and no money?"

"Someone who wanted you for yourself, instead of just for a free ride," Stephanie said frustratedly. "C'mon Mom, you gave him back his rent money!"

"His check was worthless. If I had deposited it, we would have been charged a bank fee when it bounced."

"Mom, you're missing the point," she said, feeling her anger rumbling beneath the surface like a volcano. "You let him take over—"

"It was good for me to have someone to lean on."

"What?" The fury erupted. "What have you been doing to me for the last seven years, Mom?"

"A daughter doesn't take the place of man," Mrs. Ling said.

"But you made me take the place of Daddy when he left," Stephanie snapped, clenching her hands into fists. "I had to grow up in one lousy day without finding out why, remember? I had to become the 'man' of the family, I had to get paper routes and go digging through the Salvation Army donation boxes for clothes for us, remember? And now I find out that all those miserable years weren't because Daddy didn't want *us,* they were because he didn't want *you.*"

Her mother went pale.

"I'm sorry," Stephanie said, appalled. This discussion was turning into everything she hadn't wanted it to.

Her mother looked away.

"Don't do that," she said. "Don't withdraw on me again. You owe me and Ana and Corinne more than that."

"I do not owe you my humiliation," Mrs. Ling said raggedly.

"We don't want your humiliation, Mom. All we want is our father."

"Your father doesn't exist."

"Yes he does!" Stephanie cried, crashing a fist down onto her bureau. "He lives in San Francisco with a man named Ron and he's been sending us Christmas cards . . ." Her voice cracked. "And birthday cards and letters and money and he's never stopped, even though he's

69

never, ever got even one answer back. You have to tell me what happened, Mom. I deserve to know. He's my *father.*"

Mrs. Ling remained silent.

Stephanie took a deep breath, willing herself to stay calm. "Did he cheat on you with Ron before you guys separated?"

"In his mind," Mrs. Ling whispered, sagging. Her head fell forward and her hair covered her face but it sounded like she was crying. "He told m . . . me he was in love with someone else, this . . . this *man* Ron and said he was s . . . sorry . . ." She broke into harsh sobs. "He said he had j . . . just discovered he was g . . . gay and Ron was everything he wanted and they hadn't even k . . . kissed yet. Oh, just to say it makes me ashamed, but he wanted me to know he was still honoring our m . . . marriage . . ." She caught her breath. "And then he left."

"Oh, Mom," Stephanie said, feeling a surge of compassion for the small, broken woman on the bed who had been married right out of high school to a man her father had brought home. She'd become a wife and a mother, always relying on men to take care of her and then *bam,* her world had been shattered.

But that still didn't excuse the seven-year silence.

"Tell me Stephanie, what kind of woman is so bad a wife that her husband turns to other men?" Mrs. Ling said, covering her face with her hands.

"Did Daddy say that to you?" Stephanie asked incredulously.

"No one had to say it to make it true," her mother mumbled.

"Oh, my gosh," Stephanie said with a blinding flash

of insight. "Mom, you didn't *make* Daddy gay. It had nothing to do—"

"I don't want to talk anymore," her mother said, rising.

"Wait." Stephanie whipped in front of the door. "Is *that* why you never told? Because you thought you were such a bad wife and mother that you *made* Daddy gay? Mom, Daddy's not gay because you didn't get his shirts clean enough—"

"This is not a joke," Mrs. Ling said, eyes flashing with anger. "You don't know the shame your father has left me with."

"Mom." Her mind was whirling and words crowded her throat, fighting to be spoken. "Did you cheat on Daddy?"

"No," her mother said, recoiling in horror.

"Did you steal from him?"

"Never. He was my husband."

"Did you lie to him?"

"Only when I told him the 'E' on your first report card stood for 'Excellent,' not failure," Mrs. Ling said, meeting her daughter's urgent gaze. "What is all this, Stephanie?"

"Wait." This was so, so important and if she didn't get it out now, there wouldn't be another chance. "Did you physically assault him? Did you punch, kick, bite, or pull his hair?"

"Of course not. Stephanie—"

"Were you an alcoholic? A drug abuser? A child molester? Did you scream in his face every night and tell him he was worthless?"

"No. Stephanie—"

"Did you deny him sex?" Stephanie said bluntly.

71

Mrs. Ling blushed. "Never," she mumbled, looking away.

"Then Mom," Stephanie said, crouching slightly and peering up into her mother's downcast eyes, "what makes you think you drove him away? What terrible thing did you do to make him gay?"

"I don't know!" Mrs. Ling cried, clenching her hands into fists. "I've thought of it over and over and I still don't know."

"Did you ever think that maybe it wasn't you at all?" Stephanie said, watching her mother's tear-streaked face go slack with shock. "Don't get me wrong Mom, just because I'm trying to figure this out doesn't mean everything's fine. When you and Daddy had kids, you made an unspoken promise to always take care of us and as far as I'm concerned, you both screwed-up big time."

"I never left you," Mrs. Ling said, frowning.

"Yes, you did. You were so worried about the shame of being dumped that you left me miserable for the past seven years . . ." Stephanie couldn't continue for a moment. "And I can't get any of that time back now, Mom. I was only a little kid and you and Daddy jumped ship and left me there to handle everything. That was my *childhood*, the only one I'll ever have and you know what? It sucked. You guys ruined it and you ruined Ana and Corinne's, too. You made your lives more important than anything else and we took the fall-out. And for what?"

Mrs. Ling's eyes filled with tears.

"Before you go, there's one last thing I want to tell you," Stephanie said hoarsely, turning away. "I'm gonna call Daddy."

Her mother gasped.

"Not because I'm trying to hurt you but because I have the right to talk to my father." She went to the bed and took thirty dollars from the pile of cash. "Here, take the girls to the movies. I don't know how I'm going to react when I finally hear his voice and I have no idea what he's gonna do when he hears mine. If it gets ugly, I don't want them to know." She lifted her chin. "Will you do that for me please? Now?"

Mrs. Ling searched her daughter's face, then took the money and walked silently out.

"Oh, God," Stephanie whispered. "Help."

Five

"How come *we* have to go see some lame movie an Stephanie gets to stay home?" Anastasia cranked, stomp ing down the stairs after her mother. "Man, I'd better no see anybody I know."

"Really? I hope I see *everybody* I know." Corinne gav an excited hop. "Hey, Mom, how come we have enoug money to go to the movies? I thought it cost too much.

"Why don't you just advertise how poor we are? Anastasia said, opening the front door and shoving he little sister through it. "Mom, if she's gonna be a jer the whole time, I'm staying home."

"Quit pushing me," Corinne said, darting away. "Ca we buy popcorn and drinks when we get there, Mom? want extra butter on mine."

"They don't butter the drinks, beanbag," Anastasi mocked.

"I'm not a beanbag!"

The house fell silent.

Stephanie drifted into the living room and watche from behind the curtain as her mother's car chugge away. It was drizzling again and the tires left a faint trail on the pavement.

"So," she said loudly, dropping the curtain and wandering into the kitchen. She brushed the crumbs from the table, washed the lunch dishes and put away the mustard but no matter which way she turned, the old, red wallphone with the stretched-out cord stayed in her line of vision.

The clock above the sink ticked off the passing seconds.

"I will," she said, suddenly wishing she hadn't sent the rest of her family away; this was way too huge to do alone. What if he wasn't there or worse, what if he was busy and told her to call back? Seven years had passed. She didn't even know him anymore, had only known him as a little girl, could only remember bits and pieces, flashes of light and laughter that hurt her more than any physical punishment ever could.

She closed her eyes, remembering when he'd showed her how to stand on her head and everything had come tumbling out of his pockets. He'd let her keep the jingling, silver change rolling around the floor, too.

And how, when he mowed the lawn back in those sleepy summer afternoons, she would search out a patch of cool grass and lie on her stomach, nibbling the tender shoots and waiting for him to call for the glass of lemonade at her side.

And how he'd liked Glen Campbell, of all people, and had taken her to Puget Sound and as they'd explored the shore he'd sung "Galveston" to her, only he'd substituted "Stephanie" for "Galveston" and even though the words were sad, she would never forget the way he'd smiled and scooped her up to perch on his strong shoulders . . .

"I didn't want to cry," she said, biting down on her fist. "Not now." Taking a deep, steadying breath, she ripped a paper towel from the roll and scrubbed her cheeks, welcoming the sting. "Now, I will call my father."

She pulled his last letter from her sweatshirt pocket and putting the receiver to her ear, punched out his number.

It rang. Once. Twice.

"Hello?"

Stephanie opened her mouth but nothing came out.

"Hello?" A little more impatiently.

"Can I talk to David Ling, please?" she whispered, digging her nails into her sweaty palms. Was this him? Could his voice have changed so much or was her memory faulty? His voice had been quieter, more soothing—

"Sure. Hold on." The phone clunked down.

"Oh, God," she moaned, groping for a chair. Her knees had dissolved and her entire body was trembling so bad she could barely hold the receiver. She wanted to hang up, to push the past back into the past where it could ache but not live again.

"This is David Ling."

Stephanie closed her eyes, reeling. Pain. Such pain.

"Hello?" He sounded puzzled. "Ron, there's nobody here—"

"Daddy?" she said, pressing a hand over her mouth so she wouldn't start sobbing. "It's me, Stephanie."

A heartbeat passed.

"Stephanie?" His voice went hoarse. *"My* Stephanie?"

"Yes," she said, laying her forehead down on the table. "Happy New Year, Daddy. I . . . missed you." And suddenly she was a terrified, ten-year-old girl again and she

76

couldn't stop crying but it was all right because she had finally found her father and he was there, in San Francisco and he was crying, too.

Six

"I have come to the conclusion," Janis said the next morning, joining Cassandra and Natalie out in the crowded Seven Pines courtyard, "that there is nothing more disgusting than the first day back to school after vacation."

"Nothing?" Natalie said, grinning. "What about a raccoon coat? What about people who eat tongue? What about—"

Janis sighed and hitched up the front of her peasant blouse, wishing she'd worn more than a bra underneath it. The wide neck had a tendency to dip down low because there wasn't much there to stop it. "C'mon Nat, those things fall into the Digusting Hall of Fame. *I'm* talking medium disgusting, here. Coming back to school is grosser than like, picking pimples but not as gross as—"

"This whole conversation?" Cassandra suggested pointedly.

"Hey, she started it," Natalie said, giving Janis a friendly hip bump. "So Sandifer-whatever, what's new out in that commune you call home?"

"It's not a commune . . . oh, why do I even bother to argue?" Janis said, catching Natalie's devilish expression. "Let's see, Brian came over for the first time yesterday . . ." She paused, watching Natalie. "While my parents weren't home."

"And?" Natalie said, eyes gleaming.

"And what?" Janis said, trying to look innocent.

"Did you do the deed?" Natalie said, leaning back against the brick wall and shoving her hands into her jacket pockets.

"Natalie!" Cassandra said, blushing.

"What?"

Cassandra twisted the pink quartz bracelet encircling her delicate wrist. "Don't you think that's a little personal?"

"Hey, we're all sisters and sisters share, right?" Her grin widened. "C'mon Jan, what's the deal? And don't leave anything out. I'm talking serious detail, here."

"You," Janis said, tugging up her blouse, "are a vulture."

"Yeah, yeah, whatever," Natalie said, waving her on. "So?"

"Maybe she doesn't want to talk about it," Cassandra said.

"Don't be bizarre, of course she does. Don't you, Janis?" Natalie said hopefully. "Oh, come on, you can't say anything I haven't already heard at least twice."

"Okay," Janis said, lowering her voice and stifling a grin as they leaned closer. "We were hanging out in the living room, see, and we started kissing and sort of laid down on the couch and then . . ."

"Then what?" Natalie hollered, grabbing her arm. "What?"

"Then the dogs had to go out so we took them for a

walk," Janis said, laughing at the shocked disbelief on Natalie's face. "And *then* we came back inside and my parents came home so we ate cranberry bread, only Brian didn't want any, and we talked about Harmony House— you really should come down there with me this afternoon—and then Brian left. We had a good time."

"You're lying," Natalie said, staring at her. "You're telling me you and Brian had the whole house to yourselves and the best thing you could find to do was walk the dogs?"

"Maybe not the *best* thing," Janis admitted, grinning. "But definitely the most sanitary. I mean, you haven't seen anything till you've seen *three* dogs who don't get outside in time—"

"I'm freaked," Natalie said, plopping back against the wall and wincing as her hair stuck to the bricks. "Ow. Girl, I swear I will never understand you."

"But you love me anyway, right?" Janis said, laying her head on Natalie's shoulder and beaming up at her.

"Get off me," Natalie said, laughing and twisting away.

"Cass thinks I did right, don't you, Cass?" Janis asked cheerfully, glancing into Cassandra's preoccupied face. When she didn't answer, Janis glanced at Natalie, who snorted.

"Don't mind her," Natalie said. "If she isn't dreaming about Faizon, she's worrying about her bod."

"What's wrong with her bod?" Janis asked, giving Cassandra's long, lithe dancer's build a quick once-over.

Natalie shrugged. "She thinks she's still too bony to dance because her shoulder blades and her ribs stick out. And she hasn't gotten her period since she got sick, either. I told her to tell the doctor so he can check it out but she gets all weird when it comes to talking about stuff like that. Don't you, Cass?" she added, nudging her.

80

Cassandra started. "Huh? What?"

"Never mind," Natalie said. "You just go back up onto that cloud with Faizon and let us take care of the real world."

"Don't be condescending," Cassandra said sharply. "I live in this world just like you do, Natalie, and I went through hell to make sure of it."

Whoa, Janis thought, watching as a range of emotions played across Natalie's face. Here's a kicker. Cassandra has finally decided to stick up for herself. Faizon's therapy must be working.

"Hey, sounds good to me," Natalie said after a moment, shivering as a gust of wind swept through the horseshoe-shaped courtyard. "Brr, want to wait for Maria and Steph inside?"

"Sounds good to me," Cassandra echoed, making peace.

"Hey, Nat, did you really think I'd do it with Brian so fast or was that just a joke?" Janis whispered, as Cassandra went into the building ahead of them.

Natalie gave her a long, steady look. "Just a joke," she said finally.

"I thought so," Janis said, nodding.

Stephanie signaled and turned her Ford Escort into the school. The car bounced and belatedly, she realized she'd hit the first speed bump without even noticing.

"Pay attention," she told herself but it was impossible to focus on things like speed bumps when there were so many other things to think about.

Like the fact that her father was flying up to Seattle on Saturday and she was going to see him.

Or the fact that her mother had nearly fainted when she'd told her and when Stephanie had asked about telling Ana and Corinne the truth, Mrs. Ling had turned and walked away.

"But I'm wired anyhow," Stephanie said, turning up the tape player. Aerosmith's latest blasted through the car and she rolled down her window, letting the music soar out onto the wind. "How am I ever gonna get through this week?"

Maria swung her little red Miata into a parking spot and killed the engine. She fluffed her hair, re-applied her lipstick and surveyed the parking lot. Janis's Bronco, Cassandra's BMW, Stephanie's Escort. Everyone was here already but her.

"Nice job," she muttered, slipping from the car and hurrying across the parking lot toward the courtyard. "The first day back and you don't even get here early enough to hang out." She rounded the corner and walked smack into Vanessa.

Of all people to start the day with, Maria groaned silently, summoning up an apologetic smile. She and Vanessa had been cheerleading buddies, or rather Queen Vanessa had led and Maria had followed without question until she'd met Janis and the others. Vanessa, who thought Maria's new friends were the biggest bunch of losers alive because they did things their own way, had never understood Maria's "defection" and the two hadn't talked much since. "Whoa, sorry about that," Maria said, stepping back and preparing to go around her.

"Hold up, Torres," Vanessa said, exchanging looks

with Tiffany and Donna, who flanked her like body guards. "I want to talk to you."

"Me?" Maria's stomach sank. "About what?"

Vanessa lifted her chin and narrowed her eyes. "You've been spreading lies about my boyfriend and I want you to shut up."

It took Maria a moment to figure out what she meant and when she did, a furnace-blast of anger shot through her. Vanessa was going out with Leif Walters, the huge, lumbering football player who'd taken Maria home after the Homecoming dance, tried to rape her and then dumped her out in the rain, leaving her to find her own way home. And then he'd told everyone they'd done it in the park after the dance and that she'd loved it. He'd made her feel cheap and used, like it had somehow been her fault, and if it hadn't been for her friends, she'd probably still believe it.

"Comprende, Torres?" Vanessa said, poking her in the shoulder. "I don't need you dissing my boyfriend just because he dumped you afterwards."

"Don't touch me, Vanessa," Maria said in a low, stiff voice.

Vanessa snorted and glanced at Tiffany, who looked uneasy. "She's tough now, huh? I guess you've got to be, hanging around with that bunch."

"You are *so* stupid," Maria said, scared to death inside but refusing to feed Vanessa's power. She planted her hands on her hips, imitating Natalie's "attitude" stance. "Leif Walters pinned me in his car after the Homecoming dance, drooled all over me, had to punch me in the face to make me hold still because the thought of even kissing him made me throw-up—"

"You better shut up," Vanessa said, growing red in the face.

But it was too late. There was strength in being the attacker instead of the victim and Maria intended to use it. "And when he couldn't get anything off me, he played the real big man. He split my lip and I bled all over. If you look hard enough, you'll probably find dried blood in his car. But you're *not* gonna look because you don't want to believe it." Maria's voice whipped out across the silent courtyard. "You don't want to believe that your big, fat load of a boyfriend hits girls when he doesn't get his way, do you?"

"You're so full of it," Vanessa sneered. "Everybody knows you're only doing this to get back at Leif because he's white and you want him screwed for breaking up with you."

Maria's jaw dropped, then she threw back her head and laughed. It was a ragged, incredulous laugh but it rang out over the courtyard. "Oh, *please,* you can do better than that. I'm not telling people about what Leif did to me because he's *white,* I'm telling because he's *violent.* He has a serious problem and any other girl who thinks about going out with him shouldn't have to find out the hard way. And he's not the only one, either," she said, glancing around the crowd. Several girls turned away and she made a mental note to track them down later. "There are other guys in this school who batter their girlfriends."

"And what do you think you're gonna do about it?"

"Pass it on," Maria said evenly, meeting her gaze.

"Man, you are really whacked," Vanessa said and motioning to her bookends, strode up the stairs into the building.

Maria remained where she was for a moment, weighed down by the whispers and a hundred judgmental gazes. Well, you wanted to spread the word, she thought wryly and shaking her head, padded up the steps and into the school.

Natalie opened her locker, cursing whatever had prompted her to sign up for American Lit when she could've aced something like American Vocab instead. "Now, if only they'd offered American Street," she muttered, withdrawing her book and shoving back the piles of papers and magazines ready to avalanche down on her.

An old flier, printed way back when Students Against Locker Searches had been formed, floated free and wedged beneath her boot. She stared at it for a moment, then bent and retrieved it.

"STUDENTS AGAINST LOCKER SEARCHES RALLY AT THE GREEN CAFÉ—FEATURING MUSIC BY CORRUPTING CLEO!!"

Having a band there had been her idea, a way to lure in people who otherwise might not have shown up.

"And now I'm living to regret it," she said softly. True, she might have met Edan anyway, through Maria and her brother Jesse, but a different meeting might have been less intense. We might even have hated each other or already been involved with somebody else, she thought, wincing as a pang struck her heart. No, she wasn't regretting her time with Edan . . . unless it was that it had been so short.

"*Bor*ing," she said, suddenly impatient with herself. What was she turning into anyway, some kind of spine-

less wimp who took whatever was handed out and let i
go at that? She snorted. "Ha, that'll be the day. You don'
live long in South Central if you go around thanking the
people who kick you," she said, tossing back a cloud o
spiral curls. "I'm out of practice, that's what it is. Thi
town is too damn civilized. I kicked Edan and he kicked
me back and now we're even and if that doesn't say
something about both of us, then I'll . . . I'll . . ." She
looked around, searching for something appropriately
awful to bet on and spotted Mr. Barnes, the strictest his
tory teacher in the school and one she had so far avoided
striding out of the office. "I know, I'll tell Mr. Barne
he wears a really cool toupé."

The warning bell rang.

"Hear that, Edan?" she said, wadding up the flier an
poking it back amongst her books. "I'm betting at leas
a month of Barnes' detention against the fact that yo
still like me enough to try again. What do you think o
that, boy?"

She turned and found Mr. Barnes planted behind he

"Were you talking to me?" he asked, eyeballing her.

"Uh . . . not yet," she said, grinning and jogging of

"Oh, lucky me," Janis crabbed, dropping her lunc
sack and staring around the table. "If the first day bac
to school isn't gross enough, the cafeteria ladies have t
go and barbecue up a thousand dead cows' ribs. Gee,
wonder what lucky stiff's got the head?"

"Don Corleone," Brian said, snickering and gnawin
on a bone. "No, that was a horse head, wasn't it?"

"Are you sure he was the one who got it?" Stephani
said, wiping her greasy fingers on a napkin. She'd de

cided to keep her good/bad news to herself until her father confirmed he could actually get a flight and she still didn't know how much of the story she was going to tell. Her mother's betrayal and her father's sexual preference were two things she still had to think about. "I always thought he was the one who'd *sent* it."

"You people are missing the point!" Janis hollered, plopping into a chair and folding her arms across her chest which, unfortunately, dragged down the peasant blouse's neckline and exposed a lot more skin than Brian could handle. "What?" she said, following his buggy gaze and scowling, yanked up the thin material. "Lecher. You're supposed to tell me when I'm exposed."

"Why the heck would I do that?" he asked, laughing and avoiding her good-natured swat. "I thought you were nonviolent."

"I wasn't trying to hit you, I was merely . . . waving," she said loftily, flinging back her long, blond hair and unzipping her lunch sack. "Anybody want some fruit salad?"

"No, thanks," Stephanie said, staring down at her pile of spareribs. This was the first time in seven years that she'd actually bought lunch and she was going to savor every morsel.

"Smart move," Simon drawled, sauntering up behind Janis. "Hey, Jan, tell us what deadly concoction the Sandifer-Wayne cauldron has cooked up today." He bent over her shoulder and peered into the plastic bowl. "Hmm, I think those slimy green hunks are kiwis and those mushy things looks like tangerines and those brown suckers *have* to be bananas—"

"We prefer the term African-American, thanks," Natalie interrupted, eyes gleaming.

87

"Natalie!" Cassandra gasped.

Simon turned bright red. His mouth opened, then closed like a dying fish but no sounds escaped.

Brian choked and Stephanie ducked, letting her hair swing over her face. Her shoulders were shaking.

Janis skipped around the table and wearing a wide, delighted grin, knelt in front of Natalie. "You are definitely the master and I am forever in your debt for shutting that big earwig up." She bowed low. "Consider me your most humblest servant."

"Consider the fact that Brian's looking down your shirt," Natalie said dryly, watching his head bob atop his craned neck. "You'd better give this guy some sugar, girl before he hurts himself."

"Natalie," Cassandra moaned, burying her face in her hands.

"Natalie." Simon sounded like he was strangling, "I've gotta tell you, I'm really sorry. I swear I didn't mean anything racial by it. C'mon, you know me better than that."

Natalie and Janis exchanged looks.

"Should I forgive him?" Natalie said, smirking.

"Nah, let him sweat," Janis said with a merciless smile. "I've never seen Simon squirm before and I like it."

"What do you like?" Maria asked, setting her tray down next to Stephanie's and pulling up a chair. "What did I miss?"

"Natalie and Janis are torturing Simon," Stephanie said, intrigued by the pink staining Maria's cheeks at the mention of his name. Hadn't they kissed each other on New Year's Eve and now that she thought about it, hadn't that kiss been a real sizzler, too? Then why weren't they even looking at each other?

"Want in on it?" Janis said, poking Maria. "It's okay, three can play. We'll take turns. Natalie goes first though, 'cause she's the master."

"No, I think I'll pass," Maria said lightly, scooping up a forkful of macaroni and cheese. "But don't let me stop you."

"Thanks a lot, pal," Simon said and there was an edge to his voice Stephanie had never heard before. Not that she knew Simon all that well anyway, but in the months they'd hung around together, he'd never been anything but laid back and sort of detachedly amused.

"You're welcome, *buddy*," Maria said, meeting his gaze.

Uh, oh, Stephanie thought, wanting to pick up a spare-rib and break the deadlock but afraid to move. There was a weird, crackling tension between them that—

"Sit down already, will you, Pearlstein?" Brian said, jerking up a chair and ramming it into the back of Simon's knees, forcing him to sit. "And you," he said, turning to Janis, "give it a rest for a while, okay? Let a guy eat in peace."

She looked back at him for a moment, then her mouth curved into a wicked grin. "You're so cute when you're being macho."

"Oh, no," he yodeled, burying his face in his hands.

"He just *hates* when I call him cute," she continued, leaning forward like a neighbor gossiping over a fence. Her eyes were sparkling and she looked like she was ready to explode with laughter. "But with a face and a body like that, well, I say he should be used to it by now. What do you guys think?"

"Want to move to another table?" Simon asked Brian sympathetically, withdrawing a bag of pretzel rods from his back pocket and offering him one.

"I'm thinking about it," Brian growled, glaring at Janis.

"Phooey," she said cheerfully, digging into her salad.

Stephanie watched as Simon offered the pretzels around the table. He hesitated when he got to Maria but when she reached out and took one, his expression eased and he nodded once, as if satisfied.

"You guys go ahead," Cassandra said, waving the rest of the girls on. "I'll meet you in the bathroom."

"Why, where are you going?" Natalie asked, lingering as the others wandered off.

Cassandra sighed. Leave it to her cousin. "If I had wanted you to know, don't you think I would've told you?"

"You're still mad at me for that crack I made before, aren't you?" Natalie said, eyes sparkling with mischief. "Don't lie; you looked like you were gonna fall out. Cass, it was only a joke." She snickered. "Man, that was clean. Janis's right, I *am* the master."

"Don't you think it was a little disrespectful to African-Americans?" Cassandra said, raising an eyebrow. "I mean, if someone else had said it you'd be jumping all over them."

"Well, that's the whole point. I can say it because it's my race. You can always joke about your own race, just like you can joke about your own family. It's when somebody *outside* does it that trouble starts." She grinned. "And I'm even luckier because I get to play both sides,

90

see? I mean, if Simon was saying something like 'that poached, pasty pale blob has to be—' and I jumped in and said, 'Thanks but we prefer the term 'white folks' I could *still* get away with it because it's a part of me."

"I'll never understand you," Cassandra said, shaking her head. She glanced at her watch and was dismayed to find less than ten minutes left till class. "Look, I have to go now."

"Where you going?" Natalie said brightly.

"Nowhere," Cassandra said, grinding her capped teeth.

"Oooh, then you must be going to the locker room to call Faizon," Natalie said. "I'll come too, I want to listen. I've never heard true love in action before."

"And you're not going to now," Cassandra said, trying to walk around her but Natalie kept dancing back around in front, blocking her path. "Natalie, please."

"Just tell me what you're gonna say," she coaxed. "Is it gonna be stuff like 'Oh, Faizon, I miss your kisses?' or 'I live for the moment I can be in your arms—' " She broke off, catching her cousin's brilliant blush. "Oh, no, no way. You're not really gonna say that, are you? *Nobody* really talks like that!"

"How would you know? You've never been in love!"

"Good, if I'd have to act so stupid."

"I guess I should ignore all your immature talk because you don't have any idea how great having someone like Faizon is," she finished with a small smile, pleased at her cousin's sudden silence. "Now, if you don't mind . . ." She swept around Natalie and sailed regally down the hall towards the pay phone, praying Faizon would be at the shelter to take the call.

Her parents would be at work until six. Carlton was staying after school to work on his Science Fair project

91

and Natalie was going down to Harmony House with Janis.

I just want to show him my dance studio, she told herself, feeling a quiver of excitement deep in the pit of her stomach. It's not my fault the studio's upstairs in my bedroom.

Seven

Stephanie parked in the Green Café's lot and moving quickly, swept her long, black hair back into a hairclip. Jen, her boss, was a stickler for doing things right and even made her husband Johnny, a cook, wear a hair net over the few strands he had left.

She gathered her stuff and locking up, jogged to the front door. The café's windows had steamed up again, making the people inside faint and blurry, as if they were moving through a dream.

"Hi, Steph," Lissa, the waitress said, glancing pointedly over her shoulder at Joey Giovanni, who was measuring out a section of newly laid floor. "Did you have a good time at Iron Mike's on New Year's?"

"Like you don't already know," Stephanie said, sniffing and sweeping past her to the register. Lissa had decided Stephanie and Joey made a perfect couple and had been doing everything in her power to get them together, including telling him where Stephanie was going on New Year's Eve. Joey had shown up uninvited, which hadn't sat well with Stephanie in the beginning, but when he'd apologized and went to stand alone at the bar, she'd started feeling bad and had invited him back to her table.

"Which was exactly what Lissa knew I'd do," Stephanie murmured. And it's not that I don't like Joey, she thought, slipping out of her jacket. He seems like a really good guy. I mean, anybody who can work full-time with his own parent and look happy about it is a better person than I am.

"Hey, you, Joey," Tony, his father growled, leaning over and giving Joey, who had been staring across the café at Stephanie, a poke with his tape measure. "This is the fourth time I called you; what, you've got potatoes in your ears?"

"Ah, get out of my way," Joey shot back, grabbing the tape extension and crawling across the floor. "Nine six and three quarters, okay? You happy now?"

"The more these pretty girls smile, the less work I get out of you," Tony said, dividing a charming smile between Stephanie and Lissa with an old-world courtliness that made Lissa preen and Stephanie feel like curtsying or something.

Joey's gaze met Stephanie's. "He thinks he's a comedian," he said, grinning and jerking his head toward his father.

"I think you guys are gonna get me fired," she said, trying to look stern and failing miserably. "Now, I don't know about the rest of you but I have to get back to work before Jen freaks."

"Good for you," Tony said, nodding. "C'mon Joey, time to help your old man for a while."

Joey shot Stephanie a laughing look and went back to work.

"He's great, isn't he?" Lissa murmured, stopping at

94

the register and handing Stephanie a customer tab. "I swear I haven't had this much fun since I started working here. It's gonna be really neat when they finish the renovation, you know?"

"I'm not thinking that far ahead," Stephanie said, ringing up the bill and handing her the change. Joey's laugh echoed across the café and the girls automatically turned. He and his father stood face-to-face and although it looked like they were arguing, she'd been around them long enough to know this was their way of communicating. Within seconds, they were grinning at each other and the dilemma, whatever it was, had been resolved.

"Maybe you *should* think that far ahead," Lissa said with a knowing gaze. "Unless you're totally not interested, that is."

Stephanie glanced back at Joey. His T-shirt hugged his muscled back and patches of sweat stained the navy blue cloth black. He straightened, swiping an arm across his forehead, then pulled a bandana from his back pocket and tied it around his head á la Axl Rose.

"My son, the sheik," Tony joked, eyeing the bandana. "Hey Tony Curtis, hand me that level."

They have a whole private language, Stephanie thought, wondering how it would feel to be that close to her father. To be able to tease each other and never, ever lose sight of the kind of love and mutual respect the Giovannis seemed to have.

"Well?" Lissa prodded, jingling the palmful of change.

"Man, you're nosy," Stephanie said, grinning.

"Outstanding," Lissa said, satisfied. "Go for it, girl." She hurried off to give the customer his change.

What's happening here? Stephanie wondered, toying with the diamond chip necklace Phillip had given her for her last birthday. I lose Phillip but I gain a car, my father, and now, maybe, a guy who couldn't be any nicer if he tried.

Joey glanced up, as if sensing her gaze.

Oh, what the heck, she thought and hit him with a dazzling smile that left him speechless and her with a sense of power she'd never felt before in her life.

"Wow, this is just like a real home," Natalie said, as Janis led her through Harmony House's foyer into the noisy, expanded kitchen/playroom. The floor was littered with stuffed animals and rainbow-colored blocks and several women were cuddling younger kids on their laps, rocking and reading aloud.

"It *is* a real home," Janis began.

"Yanni!" A blond, blue-eyed toddler scrambled to his feet and threw himself at her. "Yanni, Yett?"

"Hi, Jeffrey," Janis said, crouching and trying to hug him but he squirmed away. "He only loves me for my dog," she said, grinning as he skidded into the foyer and screeched in delight.

"Are you sure these kids are sick?" Natalie said. The other toddlers had abandoned their toys and crowded around Jeffrey, who had escorted in Jett and was deciding who could pet her and where. "Are you sure their parents don't want them?"

"Hard to believe, isn't it?" Janis said, sighing.

"Noog," Jeffrey burbled, taking Nguyen, his Asian roommate's arm and putting it on the top of Jett's knobby head. " 'Kay?"

Nguyen patted the dog, giggling when Jett licked him.

"So, like, Jan, what do you do here?" Natalie said,

feeling slightly uncomfortable. This was Janis's territory, she was the do-gooder in the group and to Natalie's untrained eye, it looked like everything was running pretty smoothly without their help.

"Whatever I can. I've gotten to feed some of the older kids and play with them, of course," Janis said, motioning for Natalie to follow her. "C'mon, I'll give you a tour of the rest of the place. The kids' bedrooms are upstairs."

"How many kids live here?" Natalie asked, padding up the carpeted steps. There were dreamy, pastel murals painted on the walls of the landing, clouds and unicorns and serenely beautiful angels of every ethnic background playing amongst shining, gold and silver stars. "Wow, this is really . . ." She shook her head, unable to find words for the feeling the murals gave her.

"You're better than I am," Janis said, smiling slightly. "The first time I saw it I almost started crying right in front of the kids. It's almost *too* beautiful."

"Is it supposed to be heaven?"

"I don't know," Janis said, stepping back to study the wall. "The artist said it was here to be a comfort. When you look real close, especially down at the kids' level, you start noticing all kinds of really peaceful scenes in miniature. Animals and ponds and stuff . . ." She straightened and shook back her hair. "I wanted to take some of the healthier kids out for a walk today but it's still too ugly. I wish spring would get here."

"It's only a couple of months away," Natalie said absently, staring into the closest bedroom. There was a little girl in there, sitting on the floor and doing nothing but watching them.

"Some of these kids may not be able to wait," Janis

murmured, following the direction of her gaze. "That's Hope."

"What's she doing here all alone?" Natalie said, staring at the silent child. She was a sturdy kid with caramel-brown hair, light, caramel-brown skin and dark, dark eyes.

"She's not alone. We always keep at least one staff member on each floor when the kids are split up." Janis stuck her head into another bedroom and called, "Hi. Don't mind us." She glanced at Natalie and wrinkled her nose. "Diaper changing is one thing I haven't volunteered for yet."

Natalie hardly heard her. She'd locked gazes with Hope, who glared at her with a hostility she found startling in a kid so little. "She's racially mixed, isn't she?"

"Yeah, her—"

"Quit looking at me," Hope said, scowling.

Natalie's eyes widened. "She can talk."

"Oh, yeah," Janis said wryly. "We're sorry Hope, we didn't mean to bother you. This is my friend Natalie—"

"I'm s'posed to be having quiet time," Hope said, trying to scramble up onto her bed. Her little legs were short and by the time she'd grabbed handfuls of covers and heaved herself over the edge her face was red and she was panting. "Go away."

Natalie, who had watched the agonizing ordeal, had started into the room to help but Janis had stopped her. "Don't," she'd whispered, shaking her head. "She hates to be touched. She's had some hard times, Nat. I'll tell you about them later."

Hard times? Natalie thought puzzledly.

"Very good, Hope," Janis said, applauding. "The last time I was here it took way more tries to get into bed than that. You must be growing a mile a day."

Hope plucked at the Beauty and the Beast comforter and didn't answer.

"What did you do to get quiet time?" Janis asked and to Natalie, "Quiet time's a discipline thing when they act up."

"Ripped Singha's paper dolls," Hope muttered.

"Singha's your roommate?" Natalie asked, wanting in on the conversation. There was something about this angry baby that got to her like none of the other kids had.

"Yes, dummy," Hope said, then flipped over onto her stomach and stuck her head under her pillow.

Natalie's face burned and she had the urge to stride over, yank away the pillow, and hug the child as hard as she could.

"Well, Hope's being nasty so I guess we'll leave her to her quiet time," Janis said evenly. "Come on, Nat."

Natalie hesitated. She wanted to stay and do something but she had no idea what. The kid was so prickly she was practically growing thorns. And if I can't even manage to connect with a happy kid, what makes me think I can connect with this one, she wondered, backing out of the doorway. "Bye, Hope. See you."

She and Janis went downstairs. When Natalie reached the bottom, she glanced over her shoulder in time to see a small, sturdy figure darting back into the bedroom.

"I think she likes you," Janis said, beaming. "She called Jett 'dummy' too, in the beginning and now she loves her. I *knew* bringing you here was a good idea!"

Good for who? Natalie wondered, sighing at the dark, angry eyes imprinted on her brain.

* * *

"This is my room," Cassandra said shyly, pausing in the doorway to flick on the light and motioning him inside. She looked around, trying to see through his eyes, trying to look anywhere but into his eyes for fear he'd see her true emotions. She'd been so excited when he'd said sure, he'd love to come over and see her studio that she'd gone hot, then cold, then shaky. She'd gone to the rest of her classes but hadn't really been there and had no idea how she'd made it to the shelter to pick him up without getting into an accident.

"It's very nice," Faizon said, standing beside her. "Big."

"That's because my father designed the house," she said and afraid she sounded like she was bragging, added, "He got a good price on having it built because he'd worked with the contractors before." I'm babbling, she thought wretchedly, stealing a glance at him. He was examining her framed ballet posters, recital handbills and ticket stubs, wandering across to her bureau where any minute now he'd see the small, heart-shaped jewelry box he'd given her for Christmas. He'd had "Faizon & Cassandra" written in calligraphy across the lid and she'd placed it in the spot of honor, smack in the middle of the bureau.

Oh, no, she thought, blushing. If he lifts up the lid he's going to find those dumb orange peels I brought home from the hospital because he was the one who'd peeled that orange—

"I wish I'd saved my dance programs," he said, leaning closer to study the photo on the cover of last year's program. He went still. "You're beautiful."

"Thank you," she said, forcing herself to walk up beside him. She stared at the program on the wall, knew

100

it was a photo of her on *pointe* in her ethereal pink tutu but didn't see it now. She and Faizon were standing side by side, arms touching. She could smell his crisp, clean scent and feel the heat radiating from his body. The air crackled and she knew, instinctively, that if she turned he would kiss her. And she wanted him to more than almost anything but not more than she wanted to show him the real Cassandra, not the scared, bulimic scarecrow he'd known in the hospital. She wanted that Cassandra wiped out of his mind and she wanted him to see her as she had been and would be again.

"Cass," he said.

"And this is my studio," she said, not daring to look at him. She crossed the room, feeling as if every step she took only brought them closer. She spun the dimmer switch, bringing the studio lights up from darkness to dusk, watching as the wall-to-wall mirrors reflected a dozen Faizons in white shirts and clean, faded jeans.

"This is incredible," he murmured, moving slowly across the sleek, wooden floor. "To have something like this, your own private place to dance . . ."

"I know," she said, hugging herself. "I mean, I didn't really know until you just said it."

His dark, glowing gaze met and held hers. "Will you dance for me?"

"Now?" Her voice was hoarse, her throat tight. She wanted to dance for him, *with* him, wanted to sink into him—

"Please? And then someday I'll dance for you, too. If you want me to, I mean," he added, sounding embarrassed.

"It's a deal," she said, trembling with excitement. This, *this* was what she'd been waiting for, the chance to show

101

him how she felt in the most emotionally expressive way she knew. "I'll put on my *pointe* shoes if you'll shut off the bedroom lights and put that Pat Benatar tape into the player. It's already set at the song," she added, trying to focus on changing shoes instead of the dark, shadowy room behind her and his lean, lithe figure perched eagerly on the edge of her bed. "The song's called 'Wuthering Heights' and I danced a solo to it in the last competition. I placed third."

"Good for you," he said, nodding.

"But now that we're together . . ." Her voice wobbled and she didn't bother to steady it; her heart was too full. "I think I would place first because I understand more than I did before." She rose, flexing her ankles. Oh, how wonderful it felt to be back on *pointe*. "Just remember, I'm not as good as I was before I got sick, Faizon. I still have a way to go."

"I'm with you," he murmured, smiling.

And I love you so much for that, she thought, padding to center stage. "All right."

The soft haunting music drifted into the room, weaving like a silver spell through the dimmed lights and the expectant silence. Cassandra lifted her gaze and looked into Faizon's eyes, let the fierce, yearning lyrics stir the fire in her soul. Her body was strong, powerful but her heart ached and as she disappeared into the music her arms reached for him again and again, begging to be rescued from the cold, dark moors, from spending eternity without him . . .

The music died and he was there, holding her, cradling her gently at first, allowing her to catch her breath, drying the tears on her cheeks and smoothing back the damp strands of hair clinging to her forehead.

102

The silence surrounded them like a rich, dark curtain and suddenly she was on the bed beside him, lying beside him and he was kissing her face, her mouth and she was pulling him closer, holding him with hands that would never let go. She could hear herself breathing, hear the steady rhythm of his heart and the soft, sweet sounds born deep in his throat and whispered into the hollow of her neck.

She didn't know what she was doing or how to do it but knew she wasn't going to stop. She loved him, all of him, the way his body molded to hers, the way he fumbled with their clothes, her ballet shoes, watching with wonder as she sat up to help, then easing her back down and loving her, all of her, even her poor, jutting collarbones.

"Cassandra," he said hoarsely, staring down at her. "I didn't know we were gonna . . . I mean, I don't have anything. No condoms. If we're gonna stop, we'd better stop now."

She stroked his face, shoulders, arms. He was so beautiful. "It's okay," she murmured, wishing he hadn't spoken. She pressed closer, drowning herself in him and dismissing his words. He was hers and she would be his and if this was a dream it could have only one ending. If it was real . . . "Everything'll be okay."

"But what if . . . oh, don't look at me like that," he said, groaning and burying his face in her neck.

"I love you," she said, closing her eyes.

They didn't speak again.

It hurt and she hadn't expected that. The brief pain interrupted the dreamy haze, throwing her off kilter, bringing her mind back into her body and her body back into reality.

She opened her eyes but didn't move.

"I'm sorry I hurt you," he said quietly, resting beside her. He gathered her into his arms and pressed her head to his chest where she could hear his racing heartbeat. "Are you okay?"

"Fine," she said, staring at the dimly lit studio. She had done it, made love with Faizon, crossed a line. She had given him something she could never give anyone again. Her body ached but her heart felt warm and full and at peace.

"Cassandra? Are you sorry we did it?"

"Are you?" she said, wanting to see his face when he answered but too comfortable to move.

"No." He kissed her forehead. "Cassandra?"

"What?" Did *all* guys talk so much afterwards?

"Uh . . . you said you loved me."

She hesitated. Had she done something wrong by saying it? Was saying "I love you" during lovemaking a major error? "Yes."

His entire body relaxed. "I've been waiting to hear those words since the first time I saw you," he said, tilting her chin up and gazing into her eyes. "I never thought I'd be that lucky. I love you so much, Cass. It hurts, how much I love you."

I can die now, she thought. There can't be anything better than this.

Natalie danced in the front door, belting out the refrain from Arrested Development's "People Everyday" and wishing she had someone to sing and act up with. Janis had tried but she sounded like someone who'd just slammed her hand in the door and Natalie had been forced to temporarily abandon the idea. It had stayed in her mind though, creating a need to celebrate with someone like that little kid Hope, who looked like she could use some serious fun.

"Or at least someone to hang with," Natalie said, dropping her purse and jacket to the floor. It wasn't hard to imagine her and Hope in the park, playing and dancing and singing, and it didn't even surprise her that her version of the song came out as great as Arrested Development's. This was, after all, a fantasy and why shouldn't it be a good one? And since it was running high, why not make Hope happy and healthy and bounding around like a rabbit, like a normal little kid enjoying the sunshine and the company of someone who could be a big sister.

"Natalie?"

"Hey, Cass," she said, glancing upstairs. "Why aren't you at ballet practice?"

"I didn't have to dance today," Cassandra said, retreating into the shadows. She seemed to be struggling with the buttons of her blouse and sounded slightly out of breath, like she'd been running.

Natalie narrowed her eyes, intrigued, then started up the stairs. Something was going on here. The air was sharp and Cassandra was acting like she'd just been caught with her hand in the cookie jar.

"You're home early," Cassandra said, turning and heading back towards her room. "How was Harmony House?"

"Very interesting," Natalie said, dogging her. "What've you been up to?"

Her cousin missed a step. "Nothing special," she said without turning. "I was really tired when I got home, so I just laid down for a while."

"I'll bet." Really, who did Cassandra think she was fooling, anyway? *Somebody* had been playing the game of life this afternoon and if the elaborate explanation didn't prove it, then the rumpled bed and the room's dark, heavy air did. She leaned against the doorjamb, watching as her cousin hastily smoothed the covers and plumped the pillows. "So, where is he? In the closet?"

Cassandra's head shot up. "I don't know what you're—"

"Oh c'mon Cass, give it up," Natalie said with a broad, knowing grin. "You can run that innocent mug past your parents but *I* know what I'm seeing. So." She sauntered into the room, "Where is he?"

"He left ten minutes ago," Cassandra admitted, sitting down on the edge of the bed. She met Natalie's curious gaze with wide, glowing eyes. "He loves me, Nat."

"First of all, don't go around looking at everybody like that or they'll know something's up," Natalie said, shaking her head. It wasn't only her cousin's eyes that were shining, it was her whole face. "And second, they always love you when you do the deed. You *did* do the deed, didn't you?"

"We made love," Cassandra said, hugging herself. Her face was flushed and her smile starry. "We actually did. Natalie, I never could have imagined anything like that. He was so . . . sweet and good to me. I can't imagine doing it with anybody but him, ever."

Natalie laughed, ignoring the pang squeezing her heart. Had she ever felt as great about messing with a guy? That was an easy one; no. "Well, I'm glad you had a good time."

"It was more like incredible," she said. "I've never felt so close to anybody in my whole life."

106

"Speaking of 'close,' " Natalie drawled, arching an eyebrow. "What'd you guys use?"

Cassandra looked blank. "What do you mean?"

"Oh, come on," Natalie said, smirking. "You couldn't have been *that* far out—" She broke off, going cold as her cousin flushed and looked away. "Cass."

"I . . . we . . . it just sort of happened."

Natalie's mind spun away and she clutched the bureau, waiting until she could breathe again. Black dots speckled her vision and her stomach thudded down to her feet. Oh, no, not Cassandra, the one person who had a real chance at a future. "Tell me you're kidding. Tell me you at least used a condom. Please."

"We didn't have one," Cassandra mumbled, squirming. "I told you, it just happened."

Natalie lifted a hand. When she spoke, her voice was hard and flat and took no prisoners. "Faizon just shot twenty million sperm into you and right now every single one of them is doing the only job they were put on earth to do; find an egg and get you pregnant. That's what they do, Cass. That's *all* they do." She met her cousin's stricken gaze and felt like slapping her. "What, you thought because you're 'in love' that nothing could happen? You thought because it was your first time nothing could happen?" She kicked over the wastepaper basket. "Cass, you *know* better than that. Those suckers are looking to connect with your egg and guess what? Once they do, you're screwed. Royally."

"Don't say that," Cassandra whispered, hugging herself. "Don't make it something ugly."

"I'm not," Natalie snapped, so freaked she could've punched a hole through the wall. "Sex isn't ugly but

107

stupid sex, doing it without protecting yourself . . . man, I can't believe it. What were you thinking, girl?"

"I love him," Cassandra said weakly.

"What's *that* supposed to mean? You love him, so the sperm knows not to get you pregnant? You love him, so being stupid doesn't count? What?" She stalked across the room waving her arms. "Tell me Cass, because I don't know. You love him, so using protection isn't 'natural,' it isn't . . ." She stopped, narrowing her eyes. "Using protection wasn't part of the romance-thing, was it? Getting down with a condom was too real for you, right?"

Cassandra hunched her shoulders and didn't answer.

"Well, now you've got something truly *real* to think about," Natalie said, rubbing her forehead. "Those sperm are gonna hang out for a whole day, trying to make the connection and then you've got to sit around and wait for like a month till you can buy a pregnancy kit and test yourself."

"Oh, no," Cassandra whispered.

"You've got to think of your future now," Natalie said roughly, wanting to cry. "If you're pregnant, are you gonna keep it or get an abortion? Who's gonna pay for the abortion? Are you gonna tell your parents?"

Cassandra moaned. "Stop."

"No," Natalie said, plopping down on the bed next to her. "All this comes with the territory, Cass. Getting with somebody doesn't stop when he leaves, it goes on forever. If you're pregnant, are you gonna marry him? The kid *has* to have a father there for him, Cass. I should know."

Cassandra looked at her with wide, frightened eyes.

"You don't know what it feels like when your own

108

father doesn't think you're worth sticking around for," Natalie said, gazing at the floor. "If you make a baby, you'd better plan on staying with it. Guys can't ditch anymore. We need role models for the babies, they can't just make them and walk away. We're losing our kids to the streets, Cass. Just come down to L. A. and see for yourself. And what about you? Are you gonna stop dancing to be a mom? Can you do that without resenting the kid, because the kid didn't screw up your life, you did *that* to yourself—"

Cassandra burst into tears. "All I w . . . wanted t . . . to do was l . . . love h . . . him."

"Street Lesson One," Natalie murmured, slipping an arm around her shoulders. "Love him all you want but do it with a condom."

"B . . . But we d . . . didn't have any," Cassandra cried.

"I do," Natalie said, sighing. "I'll split them with you."

"You carry c . . . condoms?" her cousin asked, stumbling over the word. "Why?"

Natalie gave her a tired smile. "Because the only one who's ever gonna protect me is me, Cass. And the only one who can protect you is you. Words don't mean anything when the deed goes down. It's all in the action and the action is protection."

"Don't tell anyone, okay Nat?" Cassandra whispered after a moment, straightening and wiping her eyes.

"Not even Faizon?"

"No," she said vehemently. "Not until I know for sure if I'm . . ." Her voice broke and she buried her face in her cousin's big, baggy sweatshirt and sobbed like a baby.

Crap, Natalie thought, feeling like crying herself.

Eight

Maria pulled into a parking space and turned off the windshield wipers, watching in dismay as sheets of rain drenched the glass.

"And of course I'm too cool to carry an umbrella," she said, trying to gauge how wet she'd get if she dashed all the way to the courtyard. Definitely soaked. She glanced at the back gym door, the same door she'd used the night of the Homecoming dance, when Leif had attacked her. She hadn't used it since then and now, at less than half the distance of the courtyard and in the pouring rain, it was looking more like a savior than a threat.

"Okay," she said, zipping her purse so she could hold it over her head. "On your mark, get set . . . *go!*"

Flinging open the door, she struggled out, slammed it, and bounded across the parking lot. It was impossible to avoid the puddles—the entire blacktop was one big lake—so she didn't even try. She reached the back door, grabbed the handle, and praying it wasn't locked, gave a hearty yank. It flew open and relieved, she shot into the

all.

she said, holding her purse out at her side.

"What a mess." Shivering, she slipped out of her streaming coat. The hall smelled dank and sweaty, like freshly used sneakers, and echoed a with rumbling thunder, which puzzled her until she stepped out into the gym, where a huge herd of guys were running laps.

"Of course," she muttered grimly, blushing as a passing senior gave her damp, clingy sweater an appreciative look. She had to get through the gym to get to the main hall but she was gonna have to run to make it untrampled.

"Hey, Torres," someone bellowed. "Move it or lose it!"

She looked across the gym to the stage, where Coach Garry stood grinning. He was a football coach, well-liked for his kidding nature almost as much as for his ability to bring the team to their fifth winning season. He'd subbed for her cheerleading coach every so often and drove everyone hard, which hadn't bothered Maria nearly as much as his tendency to stride into the girls' locker room whenever he felt like it, bellowing orders.

That's one good thing about being off the squad, she thought. No more Coach Garry locker-diving.

"Torres!" he hollered.

"I'm going," she yelled back, timing her escape. She waited until the main body of joggers had thundered past, spotting and waving at Brian, then took off after them, trying to make it out before they came around again.

"Hey, shake it baby," someone yelled.

Maria tightened her grip on the coat she had clutched to her chest and increased her pace. The door didn't seem to be getting any closer but the rumbling behind her was. Pigs, she thought, as a leering senior jogged alongside her.

111

"Want me to hold 'em up for you?" he offered, cupping both his hands and staring pointedly at her bouncing breasts.

At first she wasn't going to answer but ignoring him wasn't making him go away. He was jogging backwards in front of her, hands cupped, making a spectacle of her. Anything she said in English would only increase his amusement, so she took a deep breath and with all the scorn she could muster, gave him a disdainful onceover, letting her gaze linger on his knobby knees as she said, *"Vete a echar pulgas a otra parte."*

"Huh?" he said, frowning. "What's that mean?"

She gave him a killer look and remained silent, because the translation, *Go throw fleas somewhere else,* didn't sound nearly as nasty as the Spanish version did.

"What'd you say to me?" he demanded, turning red.

"What do you think?" she countered and slipped past him into the crowded, outer hallway. Her heart was racing, her cheeks hot with embarrassment, and she felt like storming back in there and telling Coach Garry what that jerk had said to her.

"Maria?"

She jumped, startled. There was a girl standing in front of her, a small, chunky girl with sad, cocker-spaniel eyes and wearing purple lipstick. "Yeah?"

The girl hesitated. "I wanted to talk to you but if this's a bad time . . ."

"No," Maria said hastily. "Really, it's fine. Want to walk up to my locker with me? I'd like to ditch this soggy coat."

The girl glanced over her shoulder. "Okay, but we'd better hurry. My . . . um, boyfriend likes me to meet

112

him by the courtyard in the morning when his bus gets in."

"Well, we can talk here if you want—"

"No!" the girl blurted. "I mean, if he sees me talking to you, I'm dead. Let's walk."

"You don't have to be dead, you know," Maria said carefully, as they headed for the staircase. "This *is* what you wanted to talk to me about, right? What your boyfriend does to you?"

"He doesn't really mean it," the girl said, keeping her gaze on the floor. "I just make him mad sometimes. He wouldn't do it if he didn't love me, right? I mean, if he didn't care what I did, he wouldn't get so mad when I did wrong, right?"

"What exactly does he do to you?" Maria asked, trying to go slowly.

The girl glanced behind her and finding the staircase empty, spun and lifted up the back of her shirt. Her skin was mottled with faded, green bruises. "I went to my friend's party without him and he was worried about me," she said, lowering her shirt and gazing earnestly at Maria. "Worrying about someone isn't abuse, is it? Doesn't this mean he really cares about me?"

Easy, Maria cautioned herself. "Do you have a best friend?"

"Sure. We've been friends since kinnygarden."

"Does she care about you?"

"Well, yeah. And I care about her."

"Does she beat you to show how much she cares?"

The girl looked uncertain. "Well no, but she's a girl."

"What difference does that make?"

"Well, girls don't hit."

"So then how do you know she cares about you?"

113

The girl frowned. "She's always there for me, you know? I mean, she's my best friend. We talk and laugh and cry about stuff and we hang out and she knows like, everything about me and . . . I don't know, she's just my best friend."

Maria smiled. "You're lucky to have such a good friend. Does she like your boyfriend?"

"No, she hates his guts. He hates her, too. He says she's trying to break us up and I shouldn't hang with her anymore."

"*Is* she trying to break you guys up?" Maria asked, propping her purse against the locker and fiddling with the combination.

"Well, maybe," the girl said, squirming. "She thinks he's bad for me. But she doesn't know him like I do. He's really sweet . . ." She trailed off, looking miserable. "It's a big mess."

"Let me tell you what you just said to me, okay?" Maria said quietly, turning to face the girl. "You have a friend who's stuck by you since kindergarten, who shares all the good and bad things in your life and who loves you like you're her sister, right?"

The girl nodded.

"And you have a boyfriend who says he loves you but wants you to obey him and when you don't, he hits you and tells you he's only doing it because he loves you and you should listen to what he says because it's for your own good, right?"

The girl nodded once and folded her arms across her chest.

"And does he tell you that if you break up with him, you'll never find anybody else who loves you like he does?"

114

The girl bit her lip.

"And you know that's a lie, don't you, because people loved you *before* you got with him and that won't stop once you leave him." She met the girl's frightened gaze, trying to find the right words without sounding like she was preaching. "Leif Walters hit me because I wouldn't do what he wanted. He didn't care about anyone but himself. *He* wanted what *he* wanted and if he had to use force to get it, so what. That's not love, that's brutality. When Leif hit me, it made him feel like a big man."

"But my boyfriend says—"

"Your boyfriend is using his fists to make you do what *he* wants," Maria interrupted. "He has no right to hurt you. He has no right to hit you, no matter what he says. And deep down in your heart, you know that, don't you?"

"What am I supposed to do, Maria?" the girl whispered.

Here's where it gets sticky, she thought. If I tell her to tell her parents, she may bolt. "Who else knows about this?"

"My best friend," she said. "That's it."

"You haven't told your parents."

"No!" The girl recoiled. "They'd freak big time and probably ground me or something. Oh, no, no way."

Maria nodded, understanding the girl's fear and explained how she hadn't wanted to tell her parents either because once the words were out, they could never be taken back. "But I *did* tell and even though it was hard, it helped a lot," Maria said, as the girl shook her head. "Okay, then, how about Guidance? You can talk to them in private and if you ever get comfortable with the idea, they can stay with you if you *do* decide to tell. Either

115

way, you should stop seeing your boyfriend. Believe me, you don't deserve to be beaten by anyone, especially not in the name of love."

"I guess," the girl said slowly.

"I bet your best friend'll be thrilled to have you back," Maria urged. "Seriously, do it for your own safety. And if he promises never to hit you again if you just stay with him, don't you do it. If he's hit you once, he'll do it a thousand times, maybe even until he kills you."

"He'd never do that," the girl said, shaking her head.

"I never thought Leif would punch me in the face, either," Maria said pointedly. "But it happened."

The bell rang.

"Oh, my God, I was supposed to meet his bus," the girl said, panicking.

"But—" Maria said, shocked as the girl sped away through the crowd. She stared blankly after her, wondering why, after all that, the abusive boyfriend still had the upper hand. "Maybe I'm just kidding myself," she said, sighing and slamming her locker. "She didn't even tell me his name so I could add it to the grapevine. Smooth move, Torres." She turned and began the trek down to homeroom.

Simon, standing a head above everyone else, wandered into sight and she veered towards him, wanting to tell him about her morning, when she noticed the perky brunette laughing and leaning into him with everything she had, which was plenty.

"Oh," Maria said, stopping dead.

Her reaction caused a traffic snarl and Simon looked over. Their gazes locked for no more than a heartbeat then he nodded, shot her a lazy, casual smile and bent to hear what the brunette was saying.

Well, I guess that New Year's Eve kiss wasn't as potent as I thought, Maria thought, lifting her chin and sailing past them. As far as she could tell, they hadn't even noticed.

"Pizza today," Stephanie said, thumping her tray down on the table and slipping into a chair. She leaned over, practically drooling and inhaled the rich, tangy aroma. "Mmmm."

"Hey, this's two days in a row," Natalie said, blowing a straw wrapper across the table at her. "Since when do you buy lunch?"

Stephanie hesitated, then let her smile surface. There was no use hiding it anymore, especially as of last night when she'd called him, he'd given her his incoming flight information and his word that he'd come to Seattle, even if he had to ride a bicycle to get there. She giggled at the thought. "Since I found my father and he's coming to see me this weekend."

Janis dropped her fork. *"What?"*

"Get out," Maria said delightedly.

"It's true," Stephanie said, nodding. "Can you believe it?"

"Lucky you," Natalie said quietly.

"Congratulations," Cassandra added. Her face was drawn and her eyes rimmed with dark circles.

"The heck with that," Janis cried, jumping up and hugging Stephanie. "I want details! C'mon Steph, it's been seven years with no word, what happened? Did he just like, call or what?"

Stephanie looked around the table, wondering how much to tell them. What would they think of her mother when she revealed the depths of her betrayal? And what

117

about her father; would they freak because he'd left to live with a man? Would they end up hating her parents without even knowing them? How could they help it? She'd hated them for a while and she not only knew them but *loved* them.

"Steph?" Janis said, poking her.

"Maybe it's too personal," Maria said, eyeing her. "Maybe we should just be glad and that's enough."

"Maybe you should quit giving her a way out," Janis grumbled good-naturedly. "C'mon Steph, we're really happy for you but you can't just leave us hanging like this. It's *cruel.*"

"Oh, no, here she goes," Maria said, groaning.

"If I tell you," Stephanie said slowly, "will you promise not to judge anybody? I mean, I know you will inside but don't do it on the outside, okay? I'm still trying to figure out how I feel about everything and I need to be able to do it without knowing you guys think my family's a bunch of jerks."

"I promise," Janis said immediately, holding up a Boy Scout salute and distorting it into the sign of the Evil Eye, crossed herself and sent Maria into spasms. "And besides, my family's weird as anything so I'll have no reason to talk."

"I only have half a family," Natalie said, shrugging.

"I have a huge family and half of them shouldn't be allowed to roam free," Maria offered, grinning.

"Well, okay," Stephanie said nervously and taking a bite of her cooling pizza, began her story. Her voice faltered at times, then strengthened as her friends waited silently for her to continue. Janis's eyes widened when she told how her mother had kept him a secret all those years and Natalie looked away when she told them how

118

wonderful his letters had been. She hesitated, remembering that Natalie's father was gone too, but there was no stopping now.

"So, what was the big secret?" Janis asked, tucking a strand of hair behind her ear and exposing three pairs of peace sign earrings. "Why did he leave?"

Here it was, the make or break moment. "He left because he realized he was gay," Stephanie said, holding her breath.

Maria blinked.

"Oh, whoa," Natalie said.

Cassandra simply stared at her.

"Good reason," Janis said matter-of-factly. "What about your sisters? Are they gonna see him this weekend, too?"

Stephanie looked at each of their faces. No one had run from the table, no one had laughed or looked grossed-out and if they felt that way, they were honoring her request and keeping it to themselves. "No, they don't know yet. My mother doesn't think we should rush into anything."

"I hate to be the one to tell you this, Steph, but seven years isn't exactly Speedy Gonzales," Janis said, looking puzzled when everyone broke up. "What?"

Stephanie grabbed a napkin and blotted her eyes, not sure whether she was laughing or crying but knowing that here, with her friends, either one was okay.

Cassandra left before lunch was over, mumbling something about making a phone call and ignoring Natalie's sharp look. She swept out of the cafeteria, using her ballet training to keep her head up and her shoulders straight, using every ounce of self-control she had to stop

119

herself from running right out of school and over to the shelter to find Faizon. She needed to be with him, to find some sort of balance between their beautiful love-making and the horrible consequences Natalie had jammed down her throat afterwards.

She'd lain awake almost all night, haunted by the image of twenty million sperm swimming through her body, searching every inch of her for an egg to fertilize. She'd racked her brain, trying to come up with a way to reverse time, to go back to the dark, dreamy moment when she'd said "Go ahead," so she could change her answer. The sex hadn't been the best part for her, anyway. The holding and stroking and loving was what had felt so good, his mouth on hers and hers on his. They should have just stuck with that.

Please, God, I don't want to be pregnant, she thought, leaning against the smooth, stone wall and blinking hard to disperse the tiny black dots in front of her eyes. Don't let this one mistake pull me down.

But it hadn't been a mistake, had it?

Cassandra curled her hand into a fist, trying to reject the thought but it wouldn't go away. She didn't want to think these hard, cold thoughts, didn't want her mind traveling the routes Natalie had so bluntly mapped out yesterday. She'd apologized this morning—"Sorry I went off in your face yesterday Cass, but I was seriously freaked"—which was groveling for Natalie, but even with the apology, Cassandra could barely stand looking at her. Natalie had taken a beautiful act and crushed i like a walnut, stripped away the dream and reduced it to bare facts, had made her feel small and stupid and *ig-norant* for not seeing something she should have seen and she hadn't felt ignorant since she was a child.

But it hadn't been a mistake, had it?

No, making love with Faizon hadn't been a mistake. He'd asked and she'd answered and the decision, the irresponsible decision had been both of theirs and now, now they were stuck with twenty million to one odds and those were bad, bad odds for two people who only wanted to love each other and to dance.

Maybe I'll get my period, she thought, closing her eyes and willing it to come. Maybe the bulimia just screwed up my schedule and it's gonna come any day now. I don't care if I get the worst cramps in the world and have to use a whole box of tampons, it'll be worth it. If I beg and pray and go back to ballet and dance and exercise, maybe the sperm'll die before they make contact and I'll get through this all right. And if I do, I swear on my whole family's lives that I'll never, ever do it again without using something. I swear.

She stopped at the pay phone and dropping in money, punched out the number of the men's shelter. She needed to hear his voice and know he still loved her.

"Hello, may I speak with Faizon Perry please?" she said, gripping the receiver.

"Hold on." The phone clattered and someone shouted.

Faizon's slow, rich voice came over the wire. "Cassandra?"

"Hi," she said, sagging against the wall. Her chest hurt and it was hard to breathe. "What're you doing?"

"Missing you and hoping you'd call," he murmured and it sounded like he was smiling. "And here you are. I'm getting luckier by the day."

I hope so, she thought.

Nine

"Hey, sailor," Janis said, smiling at Brian and withdrawing her muddy, flannel shirt from her locker. She had ceramics next and besides being her favorite class, it was also the only one she managed to get A's in. "Where've you been all day? You missed a really wild lunch."

"I bet," he said, shooting an amused look at the grubby smock. "Stand it up, Jan. I'll bet it's evolved enough to walk down the hall with us."

"Fie on you," she said, sniffing and shaking the grungy shirt. Dried clay blizzarded down around them.

" 'Fie on me?' " he repeated, lips twitching. "Is that some kind of medieval activist's curse or something?"

"Okay," she said agreeably, stepping out of the dust storm and draping the smock over her arm. "If you walk me to class, I'll promise not to sculpt a bust of you for the student art exhibit in the main hallway." Not that she would have anyway because every piece she molded came out looking like a skinny cow and even though there wasn't anything wrong with skinny cows, except that they needed to be fed, she didn't think Brian would appreciate being turned into one in front of the whole school. He, unlike her, had a reputation to protect. She, unlike him, didn't mind being known as the sculptor of skinny cows.

"You wouldn't," he said and then catching the gleam in her eyes, immediately backpedaled. "I mean, I think it's really great that you're an artist and all but I'd make a lousy model and you shouldn't waste your time sculpting lousy models."

"Relax," she said, twining her grubby fingers through his clean ones. "I'm not going to immortalize you in clay."

"I appreciate that," he said wryly, following her down the hallway. "I've seen your other work. You've got quite a herd going already."

"That does it," she said, stopping in front of the ceramics room. "My next project is gonna be a cow wearing a football helmet and batting its long, lush lashes—"

Brian flushed and glanced over his shoulder like he was afraid somebody was listening. "Quit that, would you? I can't help it if I have eyelashes like a girl."

"Like a girl wearing mascara," she corrected, smirking.

"I'm outta here," he said, trying to disentangle his hand from her grip. He didn't fight very hard and so he didn't get loose. Instead, he stepped back and gave her a smug look. "If you don't let me go, I'm not gonna tell you what happened in the gym this morning."

"Somebody *else* got jock itch?" Who cared what happened in the dumb, smelly gym? She hated gym and had been so purposely bad at it that when it came time to choose sides, the teachers usually let her hang on the bleachers and pretend to keep score.

"So Maria didn't tell you?" he said, arching an eyebrow.

"Maria? No, we had other stuff to talk about at lunch today." Janis yanked her hand from his. "There, you're free. Now tell me what happened."

He hesitated, looking suddenly unsure.

"C'mon Brian, you brought it up," Janis said, wrapping her arms around him and backing him into the corner. "There, now you're my prisoner. You *have* to tell me."

"It's no big deal," he said, shifting uncomfortably. "She cut through the gym this morning during laps and some of the guys made a few comments, that's all."

"What kind of comments?" Janis said, knowing full well what kind of comments they'd made. Maria had the kind of chest nobody could miss but that didn't mean those clods had the right to make fun of her.

"You know, the regular stuff. One of the guys kind of offered to be her personal bra . . ." He demonstrated, red-faced and squished back into the corner to avoid grabbing Janis.

"Get out of here," she said, staring down at his hands like they were twin slabs of fresh liver. "Nobody, not even a football player could be so disgusting."

"Well, then, it's a good thing you didn't hear what Coach Garry said," he muttered, running a hand through his hair.

"Coach Garry? What does he have to do with this?"

"Well, he was there—"

"And he didn't stop that slob from harassing Maria?"

"C'mon, he was on the other side of the gym."

"But he could see what was happening," Janis said.

"Well, yeah, but—"

124

"And what did he say?" Her blood was simmering.

"I don't think I want to tell you now," Brian said, eyeing her worriedly. "C'mon Jan, it wasn't like anybody *planned* it—"

"What did he say?"

"Crap." He sighed. "It was raining and she had on this white shirt that got wet and so you could pretty much see through it—"

"Only if you looked," Janis ground out sweetly.

"Well, most of the guys looked," he said, tugging at his collar. "And you know she's kind of like, big up there and she had to run through the place to get to the doors—"

"Get to the point, please," she said, glaring at him.

"Man," he yodeled, sweating. "Coach Garry was just like, 'Hey, they didn't bounce like that back when I was in school. I knew I should've taught girls' gym,' and some other stuff—"

"Like . . . ?"

" 'If Maria ran in front of us every morning we'd be as fast as greyhounds chasing down a rabbit,' and 'Anybody who got a handful of that—' "

"That's it," Janis snapped, whipping her smock to the floor. Ignoring the cloud of dust and Brian's subsequent coughing fit, she stomped across the hall and back, venting. "What kind of school lets a dirty old man be a role model for a bunch of guys who aren't real bright to start with?"

"Hey," Brian protested weakly. "I'm on the honor roll."

"Yeah and look where's it's gotten you," she said, scowling. "What did you do to help Maria?"

"What could I do?" he said, waving away the dust.

"Fight the whole team? C'mon Jan, they were only kidding—"

"So you think she deserved it?" Janis said ominously. "You, who freaks when I mention your eyelashes in *private?*"

"Hell, no, I don't think she deserved it," he said, glaring back at her. "Don't make me into one of the bad guys here, Jan."

"But you didn't stand up for her."

"You just don't get it, do you?" he said, exasperated. "Those guys get off on that stuff. If I'd have started something over it, there's no way they'd have believed I was doing it out of respect, they'd have twisted it around to where me and Maria were messing around and that would've started a whole *new* rumor."

"So nobody helped her," Janis said flatly.

"Listen to me, Jan. If one of those guys had touched her then yeah, I would've stepped in and too bad for everybody," Brian said, holding her stormy gaze. "But this time there was nothing I could've done without making it worse."

Janis stared at him, trying to understand this strange, guy-viewpoint and failing. Going along with things just to keep the peace was as foreign to her as slaughtering her own dinner and both were things she never wanted to experience. "Coach Garry could have ended it without making it worse."

"Yeah, he could have," Brian agreed, rubbing his forehead.

"But he didn't," Janis said. "He said things that egged you guys on, right? He made it sound like it was okay to dis a girl just because she has a big chest."

"Yeah," Brian said with a weary sigh.

126

"That's all I wanted to know." She headed for her classroom, then stopped and went back to Brian. "I'm glad you told me."

"I'm not," he said with a small smile. "I have a feeling I came out of this looking like a bum."

Janis hesitated, debating. "Not a bum exactly . . ."

"But you're disappointed," he said.

"Yeah." There wasn't any point in lying about something he already knew. "I would have felt a lot better if you'd have done something to help her. And staying quiet doesn't count," she added, touching his arm. "It's like going along with it."

He stared back at her, then lowered his head and gave her a soft kiss. "Where did I find you, anyway?"

"At a protest rally, remember?" she said, smiling.

"Thanks for offering to bring me home," Natalie said, settling back in the Miata and wedging her dripping purse between her feet. Nothing had gone right today, from the endless rain to Cassandra's freaked face to Stephanie's finding her father to the visions of Edan that kept drifting into her mind, teasing her with memories of better times.

"No problem," Maria said, creeping over the last speed bump and heading carefully out onto the main road. "I know Cass has ballet today and I couldn't leave you to the mercy of the bus."

"I'd rather have walked," Natalie muttered, tipping her head back against the seat and watching the windshield wipers do their thing. "There's nothing to do when I get home anyway."

Maria glanced over at her and when she spoke, her voice was way too innocent. "Really? Then would you mind running out to Cleo's with me for a minute? I have some time before work and I wanted to ask her when she's gonna start at Seven Pines."

Natalie went still. Slowly, she turned her head and met Maria's twinkling gaze. "You could do that on the phone."

"I could," Maria agreed, taking the road to the outskirts of town. "But what would that do for you?"

"You don't have to go all the way out there for me," Natalie said, heart thumping at the thought of seeing Edan again. She had to find a way to connect with him this time, she just *had* to.

"Well, if you don't *want* to . . ."

"No, I'll go," Natalie said, then catching Maria's knowing grin, swatted her lightly in the arm. "You're cruising, girl. You're messing with some serious explosives, here."

"No kidding," Maria said, snorting. "You guys shoot sparks."

"And we haven't done anything yet," Natalie muttered, thinking of her cousin and Faizon.

"We won't be able to stay long," Maria said, steering through a puddle. "I have to be at work soon but at least this way maybe you'll run into each other or something."

She pulled into the Parrish flower farm and crept towards the house. Edan's van was parked alongside the studio and Cleo's Jeep behind him. A beat-up Chevy was parked haphazardly across the driveway and flower farm trucks lined the lot.

"Box him in so he can't escape," Natalie said as Maria parked next to the van and switched off the engine. "I'm gonna need all the help I can get."

"You'll be okay," Maria said, throwing open her door.

128

Natalie followed her, dashing toward the house and shaking herself off on the front porch. Please let Edan answer the door, she thought, trying to fluff her bedraggled hair and wondering if she looked as rotten as she felt. Rain had trickled down her collar and her back, her boots squished when she walked and she was wearing her baggiest red sweatshirt. Of course, she thought disgustedly. I have a whole closetful of hot clothes and I end up wearing something Aunt Miriam wants to use to scrub out the toilet.

The door opened and Cleo peered out. "Hey, come on in."

Natalie's heart sank but smiling, she followed Maria into the house. "Hi, Cleo. We're like, dripping all over your floor."

"No problem," she said, shoving a sheaf of newspaper under their feet. "This is a farm, we're used to Mother Nature's frenzies." She straightened and flicked the gleaming, red hair from her eyes. "So, what brings you guys all the way out here?"

"You're the big psychic," Maria teased. "Don't you know?"

Cleo's amber eyes, so like Edan's, settled on Natalie. "There's some kind of meeting going on in the studio," she said slowly. "Edan's out there with Dusty, Tracer, and Shiloh. She and Dusty showed up together."

"I see," Natalie said. So much for seeing Edan today.

"Shiloh's still around?" Maria said annoyedly. "I was hoping the rain would drive her back to Florida. Why doesn't she just leave Edan and my brother in peace?"

"According to what I could get out of Edan, her father, the big cheese, is thinking about sponsoring one of the local bands—"

"Oh, right," Maria snapped. "So now everybody's supposed to suck up to her just because there's a rumor of another label audition? Man, what a racket."

"Yeah, she's good," Cleo said reluctantly. "Sorry, Nat."

Natalie's shrug wasn't as nonchalant as she'd wanted it to be and she turned away, staring out the door at the rain pounding down on the gravel driveway. Maybe we're just not meant to be, she thought miserably, shoving her hands into her clammy pockets. Maybe I should just give up and find somebody else.

"Oh, that reminds me," Cleo said loudly. "My parents want to go up to the cabin next weekend to ski and they said me and Edan could bring friends along if we wanted. You guys want to go?"

"You're going skiing?" Maria's voice sounded funny, like she had something scratchy caught in her throat. "Cleo—"

"I think it's time," Cleo said quietly.

Natalie turned to find the two girls hugging and when they parted, she was startled to see tears in Maria's eyes.

"Want to come with us, Natalie?" Cleo asked, smiling.

"I don't know how to ski," Natalie said, her heart picking up a wild, conga beat. Oh, to be able to spend an entire weekend living in the same house as Edan. He'll *have* to see me then, she thought. He'll have no choice. If worse comes to worse, I'll just hog the bathroom till he has to go and then—

"You don't have to ski," Cleo said, eyes sparkling. "There's lots of other things to do up in the mountains."

"Say, yes, Natalie," Maria urged. "It'll be perfect."

"Yes," Natalie said, high-fiving the two of them and thinking, Man, Edan, if you thought I was after you before, you ain't seen nothing yet.

"Excellent," Cleo said, beaming. "And if we don't mind being sardines, the cabin'll sleep at least fourteen . . . Can you guys think of anybody else who'd want to go?"

Natalie's jaw dropped. "Your parents would let you bring that many friends? Guys or girls? Are you serious?"

Cleo laughed. "I'm not saying they'll let everybody *sleep* together, but yeah, they'll go co-ed. Girls dorm, guys dorm. Everybody chips in with the cooking and stuff—"

Maria gave an excited hop. "This could be a major party!"

"As long as we fill up the place before anybody asks Shiloh along," Natalie said, folding her arms across her chest and leaning against the doorjamb. "So let's see, we have Cassandra, Faizon, Janis, Brian, Stephanie . . ."

Janis careened to a stop in front of Harmony House, nearly jumping the curb and flattening the small cluster of people under umbrellas gathered in front of the hand-painted sign. "What's going on now?" she said, rolling down her passenger window and leaning past Jett. "Hi. Can I help you guys with something?"

"No," the man closest to her said rudely, turning his back.

Okay, she thought with a dangerous smile. "Then could you tell me why you guys are standing out here in the rain, blocking the gate?"

Several people turned to look at her but no one answered.

The wind gusted, blowing rain into the Bronco. "Come

131

on Jett," she said, rolling up the window and grabbing her purse. "I'm gonna go in and call my mother. If I didn't know better I'd think they were protesting or something . . ." She fell back in the seat, stunned. "Oh, no, Brian was right. It's that stupid waste disposal box for the needles on the front porch. He *said* some of the neighbors had a problem with it. . . . What's today?" She glanced at her wrist but she wasn't wearing a watch. "Crap. I bet today's the day the truck comes to empty it, too."

Jett flattened her ears and whined.

"Come on, we have to get inside," she said, snapping Jett's lead to her collar and flinging open her door.

"See, I told you. She's that woman's daughter," someone said, staring as Janis wove through the people.

"Not in our neighborhood!" the rude man shouted.

She froze and turned, looking him square in the eye. "If you have a problem, let's sit down and talk about it. Don't stand out here harassing innocent babies for having a disease *their parents* gave them." She wheeled, taking advantage of his speechlessness, and marched into the house.

"Does my mother know what's going on out there?" she said to the volunteer skulking behind the living room curtain.

"Yes. We called and she's on her way over."

"Hallelujah," Janis said grimly, peeling off her dripping coat. She felt like swearing and only the row of solemn-eyed toddlers watching from the family room kept her quiet.

"Can they do that?" the volunteer asked nervously. "Block us off, I mean?"

"Good question," Janis said, smiling absently at Jef

frey, who had crept in and was touching Jett's wet, glistening nose. "Wait until I towel her, okay? You know, if they get really obnoxious, we can always call the c-o-p-s and hit them with demonstrating without a permit."

"Isn't that kind of drastic?"

"Yeah, and it won't win us any friends, either," Janis said, sighing and yanking a ratty old towel from her purse. "Okay Jeffrey, you want to help me dry Jett?"

Several of the other toddlers wandered over and the TV volume was turned up, drowning out the chants of "Not in our neighborhood!" echoing in from the rain.

"I can't believe I'm doing this," Stephanie murmured, eyeing herself in the bathroom mirror. Her cheeks were flushed and her eyes glowing. Reaching back, she unclipped the dreaded hair clasp and shook her head so the long, silky hair swung free. She'd have to wear the same clothes she'd had on all day but with luck and a few dabs of sandalwood oil, she wouldn't smell too much like French fries.

The bathroom door opened and Lissa's head popped in. "He's here and boy . . ." She gave a long, low wolf whistle. "If you ever get tired of him, toss him my way."

"Keep it down. He's not deaf, you know." Her fingers closed over her lipstick, an old, nearly empty tube that she'd been stretching until she had enough money to buy more (and now she finally did) and she glossed her lips. "Do I look okay?"

Lissa slipped into the room. "For work maybe, but not for a first date." She cocked her head, studying Stephanie's slim form in the mirror. "Turn around and face me." She put a hand on each side of Stephanie's scoop-neck bodysuit and pulled until the seams rested on the edges of her shoulders. "Open up a little. You're skinny, you don't look like you're trying to show off." She studied her for a moment, then brushed all of Stephanie's hair back. "There. You have a good neck. Use it."

"I do. It holds up my head," she said, staring at the broad expanse of newly exposed skin. It was only her neck, her upper chest and shoulders, things she'd normally show in the summer anyway but now, in the winter, all that pale skin made her seem strangely vulnerable.

"Where are you and Joey going?" Lissa said, watching as Stephanie swept a faint streak of blush across each cheekbone.

"Just going down to the coffeehouse," she said, closing her purse and heading for the door. "Well, wish me luck on my first post-Phillip date."

"Hey, Steph." Lissa waited until she turned. "Don't do anything I wouldn't do." She grinned and scratched her tattoo.

"Okay, so, no murder," Stephanie shot back and laughing, whisked through the door and back into the café.

Joey was standing at the counter and Lissa was right he *did* look hot. Not conventionally handsome like Brian not wildly gorgeous like Jesse or dangerously good-looking like Phillip had been, just hot in a confident, almost low-key way. His jeans fit like they were used to his movements and his bulky, maroon sweater made his brown eyes and his curly brown hair even darker.

"Hi," she said, coming up behind him and feeling bizarrely shy, tapping his arm. The muscle tensed into cement and she yanked her finger back like she'd been burned. Phillip hadn't had these kind of muscles.

"Hey, hi, Stephanie," he said smiling. "Ready to go?"

"Sure," she said, waving at Jen and Lissa and walking through the door Joey opened for her. "Thanks."

"My pleasure," he said, still smiling. "Listen, I figured that since we both have our cars, I'd drive to the coffeehouse and then when we're done I'll bring you back, you can pick up your car and I'll follow you home just to make sure you get there okay. How does that sound?"

"But isn't that a waste of time and gas for you?" Stephanie asked, eyeing him surprisedly.

"No," he said without hesitation. "It's worth it to me to make sure you get home okay, you know?"

"Oh," she said, walking with him toward his Chevy Blazer. "Uh, okay." This was *bizarre*. "Do you always do this? Follow girls home, I mean?"

He unlocked her door and held it open. "If I told you no, would you believe me?"

She looked into his face, which wasn't much higher than hers and laughed. "No. It sounded way too smooth."

"That's because I rehearsed it while I was waiting," he said, looking sheepish. "I didn't want you driving home alone and I couldn't think of any other way to say it. Are you mad?"

She shook her head. No, she wasn't mad, she was amazed that a guy who didn't even know her was so worried about her safety.

The drive to the coffeehouse went swiftly. Joey opened his cassette case and asked her to pick out some music.

"Ooh, Frank Sinatra," she said, giggling. "And who's this? Dean Martin? Whoa, you're a real headbanger, aren't you?"

"Give it a rest," he said, laughing. "Those're my father's."

135

"Sure," she teased, trailing a finger over the other tapes. "Ah, let's see. Springsteen, Springsteen, Springsteen. U2. Midnight Oil. Clapton. ZZ Top." She heaved a sigh. "Well, how does some Springsteen grab you?" She shoved the tape with "Rosalita" into the player and settled back in her seat.

"You don't like Springsteen?" Joey said, shooting her a disbelieving look. "C'mon Stephanie, he's great. He's 'The Boss.' "

She snorted, hiding a grin. His New York accent had gotten mighty thick in the last two minutes.

"Well, who do *you* like?" he asked.

"Aerosmith," she said and when his eyebrows shot up waved a fist under his nose. "Laugh and die, Joey. Aerosmith's the best."

"The Toxic Twins versus The Boss?" he said, grinning and pulling into the coffeehouse parking lot. "No contest. Total TKO. The Boss wins it every time."

"In your *dreams*," Stephanie cried, throwing open her door and sliding out before he could get around to her side. "No way."

The good-natured argument lasted through the first cup of coffee and well into the second.

"I give up," Joey said finally, falling back in his seat. "You win. Not Aerosmith, *you,* because you have a hard head."

"Thank you," Stephanie said primly, sipping her *cappucino.* "However we both know that in reality, Aerosmith is *far* superior—" She broke off, laughing at his pained expression. "Call it a draw. We'll agree to disagree, how's that?"

"You got it," he said, smiling and reaching across the

table,. touched the back of her hand. "I'm glad we're doing this."

"Yeah," she said softly, waiting until the distracting tingle had subsided to continue. "Can I ask you a question?"

"Shoot," he said.

"Your whole family moved out here from New York? Why?" The word *mafia* was on the tip of her tongue but she didn't say it. Just because somebody was a New York Italian didn't mean he was in the mob.

"What, is a New Yorker living in Washington such a weird thing?" he asked, stirring his coffee.

"Well . . . yeah. To me, at least. You're the first one I've ever met." She tucked one leg under her, awaiting his answer. "So?"

"So, my grandfather died and my mother didn't want my grandmother living all alone and she wouldn't sell her house and come back East so my parents flew out and took a look around and the house was big enough and since we weren't exactly loaded with work back in the city, we said what the hell and came out here." He shrugged, eyes twinkling, "Simple, see?"

"Oh, right," Stephanie said, making a face. "Wasn't it like, major culture shock? I mean, going from New York to the sticks?"

"Yeah, but it has its high points. Back in Brooklyn I'd probably be hanging down at Dominick's Pizzeria, keepin' company with ten girls named Angelina who all have big hairy mustaches and cook polenta and light novenas so they can get married—"

"Stop." Stephanie's face ached from laughing. "You're lying. I've seen New York girls on the news and they don't have mustaches."

137

"The ones in my neighborhood do," he said, smirking. "They grow them into handlebars and wax them. One jab from those suckers and you lose an eye. Ask my cousin, Blind Vito. He got fresh with an Angelina once and *pow,* he's on disability. Of course he had to marry her after that," he added blandly. "But it's okay because he likes polenta—"

"Stop," she said. "Please. I can't take anymore."

"Sure you can," he said, closing his strong, calloused hand over hers. His gaze was steady, his eyes dark and solemn. "You know why I didn't stay in Brooklyn and marry an Angelina, Steph?"

"Why?" she said, barely breathing. No one, not even Phillip had ever looked at her like this. There was a power in him that had nothing to do with physical muscle and everything to do with the constant, quiet strength that seemed to be as much a part of him as his smile.

"Because I think I was supposed to come to Chandler and marry you," he said simply and leaning across the table, cupped the side of her face and kissed her.

Ten

"Hey, Maria," Janis called, leaping out of her Bronco the next morning and racing across the swampy parking lot. "Wait up!"

"Hurry, it's pouring," Maria wailed, trying to cover her head with her clutch bag.

Janis splashed through a puddle, grabbed Maria's arm and the two bolted for the cover of the overhang above the gym's back entrance. "Man, what a mess. Listen, I hope you're not gonna be mad but Brian told me what happened yesterday in the gym."

"Oh, you mean that disgusting senior," Maria said, plucking her soaked pants away from her legs. "Yeah, he was a real prize."

Janis looked at her, puzzled. "What about Coach Garry?"

"What about him?" Maria asked, shoving back her hair.

"You mean you didn't hear what he said?" Janis, filled with rising indignation, blurted out everything Brian had told her. "What do you think of that?" she demanded, planting her hands on her hips. "Is he a sexist or what?

139

No wonder so many guys are messed-up if that's the message they're getting."

"I can't believe it," Maria said, looking sick. "I mean, I always thought he was kind of okay, even if he did come into the girls' locker room while we were changing."

"What?" Janis's screech echoed across the parking lot.

"Oh, yeah," Maria said, nodding. "All the time."

"Didn't anybody say anything?"

"Well, we thought it was weird but . . ." Maria shrugged. "He's a coach, you know? We figured he knew what he was doing."

"He sure did," Janis said, thinking hard. This had to stop, but how? They could report him to Guidance but then they'd lose him to an adult paper-shuffle. No, there was only one way and that was to rely on themselves. Like yesterday, with that protest group outside Harmony House; her mother had shown up and arranged a neighborhood meeting where they could sit down and discuss their differences like rational human beings. "Hey, Maria, how far are you willing to take this?"

"Why, what do you have in mind?" she said suspiciously. "You're not gonna make me run around in my underwear and lure him into a compromising position or anything, are you?"

"Yuk," Janis said, screwing her face into a hideous contortion. "I wouldn't ask my worst enemy to do that. No, I just want to know if you'd be willing to try to talk to him about it. Tell him you know what he said and you don't think it was right for him to set that kind of example and stuff. You know."

"Talk to him?" Maria repeated, frowning. "I'd almost

140

rather dance around in my drawers. I don't think he's exactly used to *talking* to girls."

"Well, he's gonna have to start somewhere and it might as well be with you."

"How come I have to do it? Why don't you come with me?"

"Because the two of us might spook him," Janis explained. "I mean, he might think I'm your witness or something and clam right up. The goal isn't to put him on the defensive, it's to get him to stop sexually harassing girls."

Maria sighed. "I suppose you want me to do this right now."

"There's no time like the present," Janis said cheerfully, taking Maria's books. "I'll wait here for you."

"What if the bell rings?"

"What if it does? I'll be here till you get back." She watched as Maria straightened her shoulders and stepped into the noisy hallway. "Yell if he jumps you," she called after her.

"What're you gonna do?" Maria shot back. "You're nonviolent, remember?"

"Oh. Well, I can run for help." She leaned against the damp wall, checking it first for mildew or jungle rot or whatever miserable fungus flourished in these tropical conditions and prepared to wait.

"Yo, baby—" one of the seniors began, spotting Maria. "Oof!"

"Sorry," Brian said, withdrawing his elbow and jogging on.

Smooth move, Maria thought, smiling her thanks and

141

striding across the wooden floor to where Coach Garry leaned against the stage. His cap was shoved back on his head, his cheeks were ruddy and his eyes sharpened as he caught sight of her.

"Back for more, Torres?" he bellowed, winking at a passing runner. "That's right guys, speed up. Every time you pass Torres you pass Go and can collect another cold shower." He grinned at Maria, who stared coldly back. "So, what can I do for you?"

Maria opened her mouth, then shut it. This was gonna be harder than she thought. Sure, she'd complained with the rest of the cheerleaders when the coach had invaded the locker room but none of them would have ever dreamed of confronting him.

"Well? Spit it out," he said impatiently.

"I don't think you should make the kind of comments about me that you made yesterday and just now," she heard herself say. "Teachers aren't supposed to say disgusting things to students. You're not even supposed to *notice* students in a . . . a . . . sexual way." Oh, God, where had that come from?

Coach Garry gaped at her, then burst out laughing. "You gotta be kidding me, Torres. C'mon, this is a joke, right?"

"No," she said stiffly, folding her arms across her chest as the runners passed, hooting and howling. "See what they just did? You didn't even stop them."

"Aw, don't get so bent out of shape," he said. "They're just showing their appreciation of a good-looking girl."

"Is that what you were doing when you made those gross comments about me yesterday?" Maria said, glaring at him.

His gaze slid away and he blew his whistle, nearly

deafening her. "Hit the showers," he bellowed and wheeling, strode away.

Furious, Maria marched through the guys, barely seeing them and back into the hallway where Janis was waiting.

"No go, huh?" Janis said sympathetically. "Well, I figured as much. Too bad, too. When we go to Phase Two on Monday, he's gonna wish he'd made peace during Phase One."

"What's Phase Two?" Maria asked, taking back her books.

"We're borrowing a Greenpeace move," Janis said, smirking. "Got an extra chain with a padlock?"

"Skiing?" Cassandra said, shooting Natalie a dubious look. They had just exited the bathroom (no period yet) and were on their way to her locker. "You don't know how to ski, do you?"

"No, but so what?" Natalie said, waving that away. "Cleo says there are tons of other things to do up there and besides," her voice turned righteous, "I think it'll be very educational for a kid from South Central to be able to explore the mountains and forests of this great land."

"Oh, boy," Cassandra groaned. "That was so corny even my parents wouldn't buy it." (Where was her period? Where, where?)

"Really? I'll have to try another angle then."

"They're never gonna believe you want to go for the scenery," Cassandra said, wondering if she'd just had a cramp. She waited but nothing else happened and her heart resumed its heavy rhythm. She couldn't understand it; she'd danced like mad yesterday and still nothing. "You might as well forget it, Nat."

Natalie's snort echoed through the crowded hallway. "Forget the chance of a lifetime without even putting up a fight? Right, I might. Oh." She stopped, eyes wide and glowing. "Boy, am I dumb. I forgot to tell you, you and Faizon were invited, too."

Cassandra froze. "What?"

"Oh, yeah, everybody's invited. Now Cass," she said, arching a mischievous eyebrow, "don't you think this trip into the mountains is an educational opportunity that can't be missed?"

A whole weekend with Faizon, Cass thought, mind racing. Her parents would never go for it, unless . . . She met her cousin's gaze. "We're not gonna mention the entire guest list, are we?"

"Only if we want to be left home," Natalie said, grinning.

"Janis was right," Cassandra said with reluctant admiration. "You really are a genius."

Natalie held up a hand. "No, I'm the *master.* Get with the program, girl."

"I'm trying," Cassandra said, wondering when Natalie, of all people, had become her hero.

What a frightening thought.

Eleven

"Hi, Mr. Garcia," Maria called, waving at her Spanish teacher, who was just stepping out of his classroom. The slight, balding man was more than her favorite teacher, he was her friend and for a while she had actually thought she was in love with him. What she'd been in love with, she'd discovered, were his ways, not him. She'd been battered by Leif, who'd wanted her physical body and soothed by Mr. Garcia, whose kindness had helped heal her spirit. *"Qué hubo?"*

"Not much," he replied in English, then catching himself, grinned and called, *"Hiciste tu tarea?"*

"Yes, I did my homework," she said, laughing because she knew he knew she was lying. She'd do her homework a minute before class started because she'd been speaking Spanish since she was a baby and his assignments were a breeze. "See you later."

Turning, she walked straight into Simon. "Whoa," she said, stepping quickly backwards. "Sorry, I didn't see you."

"No kidding," he said with a teasing smile. "You were too busy flirting with your teacher, huh Scarlett?"

She blinked, confused. He hadn't called her Scarlett since New Year's Eve, hadn't even really *talked* to her as a matter of fact and now, suddenly, everything was back to normal?

"Don't worry, I won't tell," he said, hooking a casual arm around her shoulders and steering her down the hall toward her locker. "Besides, I flirt with my media teacher all the time."

Maria found her voice. "Simon, your media teacher's older than God."

"Yeah, but you'd be surprised at the wild woman beneath that dignified exterior." His grin widened. "Or maybe you wouldn't."

"Well, you'll never know," Maria muttered. He was probably only hanging with her because the brunette he'd hooked up with had blown him off.

"I already do, remember?" he said, sliding his hand beneath her hair to the back of her neck and stepping in front to shield her as a gang of freshmen raced toward the cafeteria.

Maria glanced up at him, intrigued. How could one guy be so completely unpredictable? Did he do it on purpose or was he constantly operating on impulse? "What is it with you, anyway?"

"Be more specific," he said, dropping his hand to his side.

She felt the loss and it annoyed her. "Well, I'm not trying to be insulting but you're like, the weirdest guy I know."

"Now why would that insult me?" he asked, lips twitching.

"It shouldn't because you're proud of your weirdity,"

she said with a knowing look. "You actually work at it, don't you?"

"Oh, no," he drawled, covering his groin and his chest. "I feel so exposed."

"Stop that," she said, blushing. "C'mon Simon, you look very, very strange."

"Then I've completed another successful mission," he said and straightening up, wrapped his arms around her. "You know, if I kiss you again we could start a really intense rumor. Beauty and the Bacterial Blight, as the Sandifer-Wayne troll would say. What do you think?"

Maria hesitated, not knowing if he was serious or kidding. His arms felt good around her. They'd been there before but mostly in a friendly way. This time, though . . . "I think you're wiggin'," she said, for lack of anything better.

"So wig with me then," he said, holding her gaze.

"Why would I want to do that?" She could pull away whenever she wanted—his arms were loose around her waist—but for some reason, she didn't budge. She knew people were watching them—they *had* to be because she and Simon were in the middle of the hallway, rerouting the flow of traffic—and sooner or later, some nosy teacher was gonna notice and move in to break them up.

"Because Oprah's my patron saint," he said, smiling. "And she knows my motives are pure."

"Yeah, purely bizarre," Maria said, returning his smile. He was so cute in that laid back, grasshoppery way, all lean, lanky arms and legs, with that lazy grin and endless bag of pretzel sticks he carried everywhere. And what other guy would admit he thought Oprah was a twentieth-century oracle? So why not kiss him again, right here and now? She'd kissed worse people for worse reasons

147

and while that wasn't a good reason to kiss Simon, she didn't need a better one because . . . well, because she liked him.

"We're burning daylight, Scarlett," he murmured.

She gave him a look that made him catch his breath.

"Better watch it, Pearlstein," someone cawed.

Maria stiffened. Simon lifted his head.

Vanessa stood next to them, flanked by Tiffany and Donna. "Any guy that puts the moves on Torres gets badmouthed around the school once he dumps her," she continued, with a nasty smile. "Just thought you might want to know what you're getting into."

"Thanks for the warning, Medusa," Simon said, arching an amused eyebrow. "Oh, and by the way; your hair looks truly ravenous today. Better run up to the science lab and steal a few white mice before things get ugly."

Vanessa glanced at Tiffany, who shrugged. "Uh, it's none of your business what I do to my hair."

"And I'd love to keep it that way," he said, winking at Maria, who gurgled with laughter.

"Jerk," Vanessa said and the trio strode off.

"Darn, I don't think she likes me," Simon said mournfully.

"You are so bizarre," Maria said, leaning into him for the briefest instant, then stepping out of his arms. Their moment had passed but that didn't mean there wouldn't be another one. "Hey Simon, how'd you like to go skiing?"

"Skiing?" Stephanie and Janis repeated in unison, staring at Natalie across the lunch table. Maria, Cassandra, and the guys hadn't arrived yet, but Natalie was too excited to wait.

"Yeah, you know. Strapping slippery boards to your hoofs and sliding down a snowy hill?" she said, laughing.

"I don't know how to ski," Stephanie said.

"Neither do I," Janis said, wrinkling her nose.

"Me, neither, so what?" Natalie said, shrugging. "I'm going anyway. Cass and Faizon, too."

"Faizon? How'd he get invited?" Janis said, unzipping her lunch sack and pulling out a brown, hairy coconut, a hammer, and an icepick. Oblivious to the girls' goggled looks, she placed the pick in one of the coconut's eyes, punched it through and dribbled the milk into a cup. "I didn't know Cleo knew Faizon. Other than meeting him on New Year's Eve just like the rest of us, I mean." She poked the icepick back into the hole and handed the entire thing to Stephanie. "Now, you hold this. I'm gonna bash it with the hammer and then we can all have fresh coconut."

Stephanie's eyes widened and she tucked her hands behind her back. "I don't think so."

"C'mon, I've done this a thousand times," Janis said.

"Without hitting anyone?" Stephanie said suspiciously.

"Stephanie," Janis said, sounding very patient. "Haven't you ever heard the saying, 'No pain, no gain?' Don't be such a baby. What's one puny smashed thumb compared to fresh coconut meat?"

"Then *you* hold the coconut and *I'll* hit it with the hammer," Stephanie countered, grinning.

"She's got you there," Natalie said, laughing and shoving her chair away from the table. "Should I cover my eyes? Is this thing gonna wing out over the cafeteria like a UFO or what?"

"Maybe this isn't such a hot idea," Janis said, as Stephanie hoisted the hammer using both hands. "Forget it. You probably aim with your eyes closed. A girl could starve to death eating coconuts in this place."

"Oh, give me the stupid thing already," Natalie said, seizing the coconut and slipping the hammer from Stephanie's wobbly grip. She wedged the coconut, icepick up, between her knees and raised the hammer, aiming for a head-on collision.

"Wait," Janis said. "What about the ski trip? If you miss and shatter your knee, you won't be able to ski. Here, I'll do it." She reached over and tried to pry the coconut away but Natalie clenched her knees together, holding on.

"Leave it," she said. "I can't ski anyway."

"Look, I should be responsible for my own coconut," Janis said, yanking the icepick toward her. "C'mon, Nat. Give it back."

"Get off me, girl and let's get this over with," Natalie ground out, pressing her knees together with all her might.

The coconut gave a muffled crack and imploded. Natalie's knees clamped shut and Janis, who'd been tugging on the icepick, sprawled backwards in her chair.

"Eureka," she cried, struggling upright. "Quick Steph, stick a tray under there before the pieces hit the ground."

"People are giving us very strange looks," Stephanie said, kneeling next to Natalie and wedging a lunch tray beneath the dripping shards of coconut. "Okay, you can let go now."

Natalie opened her knees and the coconut thudded down. "Can you blame them?" she said dryly. "Now I don't know if I could stand being stuck in the mountains with Tarzan there for a whole weekend." She grinned. "But I guess Brian'll have the worst of it, right?"

Janis's head shot up. "Brian?"

"Man, I did it again," Natalie said, eyes twinkling. "Didn't I tell you guys Brian and Joey are invited too?"

"Invited where?" Brian asked, sauntering up to the table.

"Skiing," Stephanie said excitedly.

"I'm there," he said immediately.

"You know how to ski?" Janis said, surprised.

"Like a pro," he said, sitting down next to her. "From dawn till dusk. Once I hit those slopes, you'll never see me again."

"Hmmm." Janis bit her lip. "Hey, Natalie?" she said with an innocent smile. "Wanna pass me back that hammer? See this hunk of coconut, Brian? Hold it here, between your knees . . ."

There was a dull *thunk* and looking smug, he dropped the pieces he'd snapped in half with his hands back onto the tray. "There, pest. Now ditch the lethal weapon, will you?"

"Party pooper," she grumbled, shoving the hammer back into her lunchsack. "When you break your bones out there in the freezing snow, don't come crying to me. And don't expect that poor Saint Bernard with the flask of brandy to stay with you until the medics come, either because that's animal exploitation and no animal should suffer because of human stupidity."

"Oh, no, we're doomed," Natalie said, burying her face in her hands.

* * *

"You're *what?*" Jesse blurted, sitting up on the couch and staring across the room at Edan.

"We're going skiing next weekend and you're invited," Edan repeated, shooting him an amused look. "Been a while, huh?"

Jesse croaked something unintelligible and shut his mouth, trying to regroup. It had been *more* than a while; it had been three years because the last time they'd gone as a group to the cabin, Cleo had died in the accident. The Parrishes had been back up there since of course, mostly in the summer though and mostly to fish, not ski and they'd asked him along each time but he'd always had something else he'd had to do. And now Edan wanted him to go back to ski?

"According to my sister, it's gonna be a major do," Edan said, running a hand through his tawny hair and watching Bugs Bunny getting a manicure. "She's invited, like, the whole world."

"What do you mean, 'she's invited'? She's going too?"

"Well, yeah," Edan said, grinning. "Seems it was her big idea. She's asked your sister—"

"Maria knows about this?"

"Yeah she knows. Her, my sister, and Natalie." He cleared his throat. "They seem to be partners in crime these days. We're looking at, like, fourteen people including my parents. Man."

Jesse felt like somebody had decked him. His brain had ground into low gear and didn't seem to be processing any information other than the fact that Cleo Parrish was going to make him go back into the mountains to face what he'd done to her so long ago. "I don't think I can go," he said hoarsely.

Edan snorted. "Yeah, you can and you're gonna. You're

not bailing on me this time, bud. No way am I gonna spend the whole weekend hanging with our little sisters' friends."

"What about Natalie?" Jesse said, gathering his tangled hair back into a ponytail and shaking it free. Bugs Bunny was getting on his nerves and he groped for the remote, lowering the volume.

"We're gonna have to play that one by ear," Edan said.

Oh, man, Jesse thought, slumping back against the cushions. I can't do this, I can't be stuck in that cabin with her for two whole days. It's hard enough dealing with her here, there's no way I can go back up there. It's the place she *died,* for Christ's sake. Why would anybody want to go back to the place they'd died? The absurdity of the thought hit him and he laughed but there was no real humor in the sound. Who, besides Cleo, had ever had the chance to revisit the place they'd died at, anyway?

And who else but Cleo would return with her killer, too?

He shivered. Don't be stupid, you're not her killer. You were just some dumb, big-mouthed jerk who ragged on her about not being able to ski. You didn't mean anything by it; kids say crap like that all the time. You didn't know she'd take you up on it and you definitely didn't know she'd hit a tree. C'mon Jess, ease down, okay?

"It's gonna be something," Edan mused, shaking his head.

"Then why don't you just stay home?" Jesse said.

His mouth curved into a rueful grin. "Good question."

"We're having a neighborhood meeting tomorrow," Janis said, leading Natalie into Harmony House. "Some

153

people have a problem with the fact that a waste disposal truck comes through and picks up the used needles and stuff."

"Really?" Natalie said, shrugging out of her coat and nearly sending the vase of fresh carnations on the foyer shelf to the floor. "Whoa, careful. Why does it bother them? I mean, is there a big skull and crossbones on the truck or something?"

"No." Janis waved into the playroom at the kids. "No, sorry. No Jett today. What? Oh . . . uh, she has a tummy ache."

"Liar," Natalie whispered, grinning.

"Well, she probably does by now," Janis said, straightening the vase. "Luna and Topaz hate going to the vet, so I don't see why Jett would be any different. And my mother had to take her into Seattle for the check-up, too because the Chandler vets might have recognized her."

"So, what do you think they'd do if they did?" Natalie asked absently, peering up the stairway. Had a shadow flitted past Hope's doorway or had she just imagined it?

"I don't know but I'm not willing to find out," Janis said, setting her chin. "Jett's with us now and that's the end of it."

There, Natalie thought, catching a glimpse of Hope peeking out of the room. "I'm gonna run up and say hi to Hope, okay?"

"Check out the little plastic animal vases full of daisies in the kids' rooms while you're there," Janis called after her. "Your . . . uh, *friend* Edan donated them and he's been keeping them full of free flowers."

Natalie stopped and looked down into Janis's twinkling, blue eyes. "I didn't even know he knew about this place."

154

"Well, he does. He's brought daisies, carnations, roses on the day we opened, the whole nine yards. All on the house, too. You know what he told my mother? That when spring comes he'd bring us some rose bushes from—"

" 'Edan's Garden?' " Natalie said, gripping the bannister.

Janis nodded enthusiastically. "And they have a really cool slogan, too. 'Who loves a garden—' "

" '—still his Eden keeps,' " she murmured, looking away.

"I think that's beautiful," Janis said.

Natalie's chest constricted. It *was* beautiful but she hadn't thought so when Edan had quoted it to her. She'd been so freaked that he'd wanted to show her around the flower farm instead of get with her on the couch in the studio that she'd mocked his slogans, dissed his roses and pretty much screwed things up.

"I love it when guys are into things like flowers and stuff," Janis continued, toying with one of the daisies. "The only plant Brian can identify is poison ivy." She chuckled. "Well, spring'll be here soon and I'll fix that."

"I'm gonna go see Hope now," Natalie said quietly. She had news for Janis; *she* couldn't even identify poison ivy.

"He's here!" Corinne shouted, cannonballing into Stephanie's bedroom. "He just pulled into the driveway! Ooh, you look nice."

"Thanks," Stephanie said nervously, smoothing her cashmere sweater. Phillip had given it to her as a birthday gift and it was the nicest thing she owned. I hope Joey's

155

family doesn't think I'm trying to show off, she thought, turning in front of the mirror to make sure her hair was lying evenly down her back.

She still couldn't believe how quickly things were happening. She was scheduled to meet her father at his hotel in Seattle tomorrow and when she'd asked Jen for the weekend off, the first free time she'd requested since she'd started working there, Jen had thrown tonight in, too. Joey had heard and immediately invited her over to his house for dinner.

What the heck is going on, she wondered, staring at her reflection. When I said I wanted to start the New Year doing new things, I had no idea I'd be taken so seriously.

The doorbell rang.

"That's him!" Corinne shrieked, catapulting out of the room.

She's more excited than I am and she doesn't even know about our father yet, Stephanie thought, dabbing sandalwood oil behind her ears and recapping the bottle. Okay, girl, here you go.

Joey was kneeling in the foyer, examining the base of the wrought iron bannister. Her mother was standing next to him, Corinne hanging over him, and even Anastasia had stirred and was watching him from over the back of the living room couch.

"I don't think you have anything to worry about, Mrs. Ling," he said. "Those screws are good and solid."

"Well, if you're sure . . ." Mrs. Ling said uncertainly.

"Mom," Stephanie said, irritated. "He came to pick me up, not repair the railing. Hi, Joey."

"Hi, Steph and hey, it's okay. I don't mind helping out when I can." The smile he gave her was so openly admiring that Corinne went off into a fit of moist giggles and had to be hauled away by a way cool Anastasia. "Ready?"

"Yes." Honestly, what kind of first impression had her family given him? Her mother hit him up for free labor, her one sister couldn't stop laughing, and the other had on so much blue eyeshadow she looked like she'd frozen to death. "Bye, guys."

"Nice meeting you," Joey said, winking at Corinne, who was watching from the kitchen and sending her back into hysterics.

"I think she likes you," Stephanie said, walking to his truck.

"Do *you* like me?" His smile was casual but his eyes anxious.

"What, you think I go to dinner with every builder who asks me?" she teased, too wired about seeing her father tomorrow to get into any deep conversations.

"Do a lot of them ask?"

Stephanie laughed. "Come on, let's go. You said your parents eat promptly at six and if we're late, we're DOA, remember?"

"Yeah but they'll wait because they know how important this is to me," he said. "I told them all about you, Steph."

But fifteen minutes later, when Stephanie stepped into the Giovanni house and saw the frozen shock on his mother and grandmother's faces, she realized he had forgotten to tell them one thing.

Twelve

"Ma, Gran, this is Stephanie," Joey said proudly, hooking his arm around her shoulders and drawing her forward. "Steph, this is my mother and my grandmother."

"Hi," Stephanie said, cheeks burning.

The old lady jabbed a gnarled finger into Mrs. Giovanni's plump waist and rattled off something in Italian, glancing from Joey to Stephanie and back.

"Of course she speaks English," Joey said, rolling his eyes and shooting Stephanie an amused look. "My grandmother's surprised you speak English so well. She thought maybe you just got off the boat or something."

Stephanie didn't know what to say.

"Don't take it personal," he said, smiling down at her. "Gran's been here for forty years and she still doesn't speak English too well. She's the one who just got off the boat, you know?"

"Hello, Stephanie," Tony Giovanni said, coming into the room. His hair was freshly combed and he'd changed into a white, button-down shirt. "Glad you could make it."

"Hi, Tony, thanks," Stephanie said, ignoring the star-

158

tled look his wife shot her at the use of his first name. Too bad, she thought defiantly. He told me to call him Tony and I'm going to.

"So, Ma, wasn't I right? Isn't she beautiful?" Joey said, nudging his mother and beaming at Stephanie.

"Oh, yes," Mrs. Giovanni said a trifle nervously. "We're having macaroni tonight, nothing fancy I'm afraid because Joey didn't give me much notice . . ."

"Macaroni is fine," Stephanie said, shooting him a quick scowl which he cheerfully blew off.

"Ahh, don't listen to my mother. She says that no matter when I tell her company's coming," he said, laughing. "Believe me, her macaroni's great. You're gonna love it."

"I'm sure I will," Stephanie said, forcing a stiff smile. Mrs. Giovanni was staring at her like there was something on her mind and although Stephanie dreaded it, she met the woman's gaze and gave her an expectant look.

"This is going to sound silly," Mrs. Giovanni said, flustered. "I . . . Joey . . . he never said you were . . . I mean, we naturally thought you were Italian and so I didn't go out of my way to . . ." She took a deep breath and blurted, "We don't have any chopsticks."

Stephanie blinked.

Joey burst out laughing. "Ma," he shook his head, "if I told you once, I told you a hundred times, Stephanie's an American. She was *born* here. C'mon, would you?"

"Well, I don't think it was such a stupid question," Mrs. Giovanni said, bustling into the kitchen. "If she was raised traditional like my mother raised me, then maybe she would use chopsticks. How am I supposed to know unless I ask, right, Stephanie?"

"Oh, sure," Stephanie said, biting her tongue.

"I mean, I don't know what the Chinese do in their culture—"

They don't ask rude questions, Stephanie thought.

"Ma, I told you, she's American," Joey said with good-natured exasperation. He glanced at Stephanie and shrugged. "See? It goes in one ear and right out the other."

That's because there's nothing stopping it in between, Stephanie thought, trying to keep even the tiniest trace of anger from her expression. Okay, so the Giovanni women had cast her into a stereotype and okay, they didn't seem to be past it yet. Hadn't she done the same thing to Joey when she'd first heard he was a New York Italian? The first thing that had come into her mind was the mob. So, if she'd been guilty of stereotyping him, why did she feel so defensive about being stereotyped herself?

"How about something to drink, Stephanie?" Tony said. "We have Coke, Sprite, *vino*—"

"Tea," Mrs. Giovanni called from the kitchen.

"Soda is fine," Stephanie said.

"Make it two," Joey said, grinning at his father.

"What do I look like, a waiter?" Tony grumbled.

"So, Stephanie," Mrs. Giovanni said brightly, sticking her head into the doorway. "Isn't the Chinese New Year coming soon?"

"I have no idea," Stephanie said, gritting her teeth "We celebrated New Year's on January first just like everybody else."

"Ma, I told you, she's—"

The old lady sniffed the air and snapping something windmilled her arms, and toddled off.

"C'mon Steph," Joey said, putting his hands on he

160

waist and steering her into the dining room. "Time to eat."

"Great," Stephanie said, nodding.

This was going to be a long night.

But to Stephanie's surprise, once they began to eat the conversation took a turn for the better. Joey and his father got into a good-natured argument over the pitch of the Green Café's floor and the old lady knotted her rosary and seemed to be having a remarkably long, mumbled discussion with Jesus.

"You know Stephanie, I don't want you to get the wrong idea about us," Mrs. Giovanni said, patting her arm and shoveling a spoonful of macaroni onto her plate. "Believe me, I know how hard it is to mix with someone else's culture." She leaned closer and lowered her voice. "I kept company with a Hungarian boy once, nice enough fella except that he spit when he talked, but God knows, it could have been worse." She broke off, grinning conspiratorially as Stephanie burst out laughing. "Anyway, the first time I went to meet his parents they were gathered around this . . . this fire in a barrel in the backyard, burning up a hunk of bacon and letting the fat drip onto rye bread and then they were *eating* it. Can you just feel you're arteries clogging as we speak?"

"Were they eating it because they were really poor?" Stephanie asked.

"That's what I said!" Mrs. Giovanni crowed, slapping her hand down onto the table. "And my God, when I said it I thought they were going to roast *me* over that fire. The fella I was seeing nearly had a heart attack and his mother let loose with this string of words I couldn't make heads or tails of and it turns out that this bacon-bread was a real Hungarian delicacy and I'd just insulted centuries of tradition. So you see why I have to ask?"

"I guess," Stephanie said. A part of her didn't but another part of her understood that although being backed into an ethnic corner was insulting and frustrating, to Mrs. Giovanni, it was a place to start. Not that it's right, Stephanie thought, mopping up the extra sauce on her plate with a chunk of bread. Before I'm anything else, I'm just a seventeen-year-old girl and to me, *that's* the logical place to start.

"Hey," Joey said, squeezing her hand. "You okay?"

"Yeah," she said with a small smile.

"Ready to marry me yet?"

Blushing and at a loss, she seized the macaroni dish and plopped a heaping spoonful onto his plate. "Eat," she said.

"You, me, and six beautiful kids," he murmured, shooting her a sparkling look. "Just say the word, Steph, and you got it."

"Eat," she repeated.

"You'd make a great Italian mother," he said and dug in.

Stephanie glanced up, met Mrs. Giovanni's speculative look and grabbing her fork, attacked her remaining pasta.

Natalie was rooting through her closet, trying to figure out what she was supposed to wear on a ski trip when she heard the bathroom door squeak open. Jumping up, she bolted across the room and out into the hallway in time to see her cousin exiting the bathroom. "Cass," she hissed. "Any sign yet?"

"No," Cassandra said without turning. "If you hear any weird sounds tonight, it's only me in there dancing."

Natalie bit her lip. "Well, good luck."

"Thanks," Cassandra whispered and disappeared into her room.

Thirteen

The air in the Ford Escort was too thick to breathe,
so Stephanie rolled down her window, letting the cold,
damp wind sweep in and clear out more than the heat.

"Oh, gosh, did I remember everything?" she mumbled,
ticking them off on her fingers as she drove.

The address of her father's hotel.

A camera she'd borrowed from Joey without telling
him why. Well, she'd told him she'd be seeing her father
but not why he'd left in the first place.

Her deodorant, which she'd re-applied at every red
light from Chandler to Seattle, regardless of the looks
sent her way.

School pictures from each of his daughters for every
single year since he'd left. Pictures of Stephanie and Phillip, photos clipped from the Chandler News when
Stephanie and her new friends had formed SALS to protest the locker searches.

And, most nerve-wracking, several of her creative
writing stories carrying bright red A+'s and featuring her
brave, bold heroine Frances, who never let anybody take
advantage of her and who protected what she loved.

These stories were more than just class assignments; they were, she now realized, her own quiet little way of protesting her life.

Frances was a woman who fought for her rights.

She would never, ever have abandoned her family, no matter what.

Frances didn't dither or flutter. She would never have let something like homosexuality shame her into a seven-year silence.

She was everything Stephanie had wanted to be and everything she had wanted her parents to be.

She was a long, silent cry for help.

Stephanie's stomach growled, reminding her she'd been too nervous to eat breakfast and that it was now past lunchtime. She was meeting her father at his hotel and once they got past the greeting, whatever that was gonna be (besides terrifying), maybe they'd go out to eat.

Maybe we'll walk down to the Pike Place Market like we did once before and eat at the Athenian Inn and I can have one of those shrimp salad sandwiches that ooze out all over—

She flicked on her signal light and glancing into her rearview mirror, turned into the hotel parking lot.

She was here.

"I'd like to thank you all for coming," Zoe Sandifer-Wayne said, giving the sullen sprinkling of people a serene smile. "I'm confident we can work out a reasonable compromise."

"I don't want a compromise, I want that place shut down," a man somewhere behind Janis grumbled.

She started to turn but her father stopped her.

"Low key, remember?" he whispered. "We're not here to antagonize, we're here to make sure Harmony House stays open."

"This is so stupid," Janis whispered back, managing to glare over her shoulder in the grumbler's direction. He looked like the rude man from the other day and if her father hadn't been there, well . . . "If they had a problem with Harmony House, why didn't they say so before we opened it? It took us a thousand years to finally *get* the funding—"

"Shhh," the woman behind Janis hissed, poking her. "Have a little respect for the speaker, please."

Janis narrowed her eyes, but one glance at her father kept her still. Only for you, Mom, she thought. Only for you, and those kids will I keep my big trap shut.

"Anyone who has an issue they'd like to address or a comment they'd like to make will have three minutes at the mike," Zoe continued. "Any questions you have will be answered and my sincere hope is that when we leave today, we'll leave with peace in our hearts and a smile for all the children who call Harmony House their home. Now, is there anyone who'd like to be first?"

Five people shot up.

"I think we can pretty much forget the peace part," Janis muttered, folding her arms across her chest. I wish she'd let me bring a couple of the kids down, she thought. It's easy to hate someone when they don't have a name or a face. . . . She straightened and ignoring her father's suddenly suspicious look, started plotting. "Just in case," she whispered, nodding.

Knees shaking, Stephanie crossed the spotless, gleaming lobby to the elevators. The elevator operator, a solemn man in a uniform, asked her what floor she wanted but she was too apprehensive to speak and merely thrust the paper with the room number written on it into his hand.

"Nine-twelve it is," the man said as the doors whisked shut.

I'm gonna throw-up, she thought, as the elevator began its smooth ascent. Her stomach was tighter than a fist and her mind reeling. I can't do this, it's been too long. I'm not a little girl anymore, I grew up while he was gone and one lousy hug isn't gonna be able to make up for—

The door *shushed* open.

"Ninth floor," the operator said. "Nine-twelve is at the end of the hall."

Stephanie couldn't move, couldn't even open her mouth to say, "Go back, I changed my mind." Couldn't do anything but stare at the slim man with the glasses and graying temples gazing back at her from the hallway, staring back and speaking, yes, he was calling her name and suddenly someone was crying "Daddy," in tiny, soundless whispers but it couldn't have been her because she had grown up while he was gone and would never, ever have gone straight into his open arms like a little girl coming out of a nightmare . . .

"They're all crabbing about the exact same things," Janis whispered, elbowing her father and frowning at the person leaving the mike. "The Harmony House sign is supposedly lowering their property values—like they could really *get* any lower in this economy, why do they think we were able to grab Harmony House at such a great deal?—and the waste disposal truck freaks them out. And they're not even listening to what Mom says, either. I mean, she's *trying* to work with them—"

"I wish she'd have let me sit up there with her," Trent said, pushing his round glasses further up onto his nose. "I think she relied too much on reaching them with reason and didn't take their fears into account. Just mentioning the HIV virus sends people to their knees and the thought of housing infected people in their neighborhood, even if they *are* only kids, terrifies them."

"Dad, the waste disposal box isn't gonna jump off the porch and chase them," Janis said cxasperatedly. "It's only a locked box full of used needles and stuff. What do they want us to do, dump it in the lake? We're getting rid of the stuff in the most responsible way possible and the truck that picks it up isn't even labeled!"

"Don't waste your breath. Your mother's pointed the same thing out six times and it hasn't even made a dent."

Janis chewed her lip, thinking hard. She understood their fear of the HIV virus—heck, only people in serious denial wouldn't be afraid of it—but they weren't opening their minds far enough to get past that fear. The virus couldn't be caught by breathing, living in the same neighborhood, or smiling at someone who was infected. The simplest part of HIV was also the scariest; it *could* be caught by anyone who had body fluids, which meant everyone was a potential victim and *that* was what freaked them out. They didn't see Harmony House's kids as individuals, they saw them as nameless, faceless, anonymous infections.

And that was the first thing that had to change.

"Where are you going?" Trent asked suspiciously when Janis bounded to her feet.

"To the bathroom," she said blandly and strode out into the Community Center's main hallway and straight to the first pay phone she spotted.

"Harmony House," the volunteer answered cheerfully.

Quickly, Janis outlined the situation. "Has the nurse been through today?"

"Been and gone," the volunteer said. "She said most of the kids have stabilized beautifully and some, like Jeffrey, have bloomed. She said, and I quote, 'It's remarkable what a little love can do for a child.'"

Janis's throat tightened. "That corks it. Can you have say, Jeffrey and Gabriel and—"

"How about Hope and Singha? The four of them have a wicked case of cabin fever and the nurse said it'd be okay to get them out into the fresh air for a while."

"Excellent. I'll be there in seven minutes," Janis said firmly, hanging up.

It was time to show the neighborhood why Harmony House had to stay open.

"Where were you going?" Stephanie asked, when she and her father had calmed down enough to speak. They hadn't been loud—the greeting had happened in near silence—but the air was thick with emotion and the elevator operator had tactfully closed the doors and whisked himself away.

"Down to the lobby to wait for you," David Ling said, wiping his eyes. "I couldn't wait up here alone any longer."

Stephanie's laugh caught in her throat. "Dad, it's been more than seven years. One more half-hour—"

"Was too long," he said, gazing at her in wonder. "My first born daughter has become a beautiful young woman. I feel so cheated that I've missed it."

And that, Stephanie thought, is the whole thing in a nutshell. "We've all been cheated, Dad and I have to tell you . . . it makes me really, really mad." Her voice was shaking, she was scared he'd be disappointed or defensive, that he'd blow off her pain and rush to justify himself but he remained silent, watching her. "I know you guys had your reasons or whatever but the bottom line was that you went off to start your new life and Mom just folded in on herself and there were no parents left for us. Parents aren't supposed to do that to children."

He nodded, acknowledging and accepting her anger. "I have a lot to make up to you."

"No," she said abruptly, having thought all this out last night while she laid awake, stomach churning with macaroni and nerves. "The past can't be changed, Dad. No matter what happens now, the fact that me, Ana, and Corinne grew up with you being gone and Mom being a basket case will *always* remain a fact and that *fact* is a major part of why we're the way we are today."

His eyes were tinged with sadness and something more, something she couldn't identify.

"So whatever happens now, whether it's good or bad or maybe even nothing at all . . ." She had to stop. The thought of losing him twice hurt more than she thought possible. "It can't be to make up for the past. We're gonna have to figure out what kind of family we can be *today* because we definitely can't be the family we were yesterday." She waited, hands clasped and chin set, pray-

170

ing she wouldn't cry, praying he wouldn't send her away for ruining their first moments together but having to risk it. She had lived too long with silence to surrender to it again.

"You say the things that need saying," he said quietly. "Not everyone can do that. I look forward to getting to know the woman my daughter has become."

How bizarre, Stephanie thought, passing a shaky hand across her forehead. I think I just turned into Frances.

"We can start with lunch," her father said, glancing at his watch. "Would you like to go back to the Athenian Inn?"

"No, let's go somewhere new," she said and leaning past him, pressed the elevator button.

"Neutral turf?"

"Fresh start," she corrected, smiling. "And I'll treat."

"Okay, guys, hold hands," Janis said, setting Jeffrey down in front of the Community Center and adjusting his knitted hat. His blue eyes were sparkling, his cheeks bright from the chill air and he hadn't stopped babbling since they'd left Harmony House. Hope, on the other hand, had asked one question, "Natalie, too?" and when Janis had said no, Natalie wasn't coming, Hope's eyes had grown stormy and her face had screwed itself into a fierce pout. "Are we all here?"

"Present and accounted for," the volunteer said, taking Singha and Gabriel's hands.

"Then let's roll," Janis said, holding open the door and ushering through the four bundled-up kids. She had mixed feelings about doing this; her mother would probably brain her for using the kids to make a point but if

171

the neighbors never *saw* who lived in Harmony House, how could they ever empathize with them? Janis, who considered herself a veteran activist, knew darn well that it was much easier to blow something off if you didn't have to look it in the eye.

"What's our plan?" the volunteer asked, pausing outside the door. The rude man was at the mike, droning on about property values and the Harmony House sign and glaring at Zoe.

"We don't have one," Janis said, staring at her mother. She looked drained and just about ready to cry. "C'mon, let's go. My father's sitting up front." She opened the door and stepped into the meeting room, meeting her mother's stunned gaze.

"Janis!" she cried, rising in one swift, angry movement.

"Zoo!" Jeffrey shouted, spotting his beloved Zoe and yanking his hand from Janis's, raced across the room and threw himself at her. "Zoo, Zoo! Up!"

Several of the audience chuckled and Zoe bent and hoisted Jeffrey into her arms. He wrapped his arms around her neck and gave her a smacking kiss on the cheek, then giggling, buried his face in her neck.

A low "Awwww" swept through the small crowd.

"You'd think this kid had a script or something," the volunteer whispered. "Did you know this was going to happen?"

"Not in my wildest dreams," Janis said, releasing the other children as they tugged away and skipped across the room to Zoe. She watched as they crowded around vying for and receiving hugs and kisses and she realized for the first time ever, that the same woman she called Mom was a mom to these kids, too.

"Janis," Zoe called. "Will you come up here, please?"

"C'mon, Yanni," Jeffrey shouted, zooming back to Janis and grabbing her hand. "C'mon Zoo."

"I'm coming," Janis said, trying to laugh past the lump in her throat and letting him lead her to the front of the room. I'm dead, she thought, catching the look in her mother's eyes.

"I apologize for the interruption," Zoe said, removing Singha's curious hand from the microphone, which earned chuckles from several grandmotherly-looking women. "This is my daughter Janis and apparently, she'd like to make a brief statement."

Janis's jaw dropped. "Huh?"

"You have the floor," Zoe said, smiling and backing away.

Shocked, Janis looked out over the sea of pale, mercifully blurred faces. Her body had gone numb and her brain blank.

"This is Jeffrey," she heard someone say and was shocked to find out it was her. "This is Gabriel and Singha and Hope," she said, touching each of the children gathered around her legs.

"Hi," Jeffrey piped, waving at Trent Sandifer-Wayne.

Several people laughed. All of them smiled.

"These are four of our Harmony House kids," Janis continued, as the place erupted in whispers. "We have seven more. They lived in the hospital until Harmony House opened because there was nowhere else for them to go." She hesitated, debating how much to say in front of the kids. "Once they were diagnosed, their biological parents disappeared."

"How could somebody do that?" one woman muttered angrily.

173

"All our children were infected in *utero*," Janis said, trying hard to use words the kids wouldn't understand. "Their mothers were HIV positive and passed it on to them before birth. These kids were alone but now they have Harmony House, which is their home and they have us, the staff and the volunteers and my mother and father, and we're their family. *Family* is what Harmony House is about. Not signs—if the sign is lowering your property value we'll take it down, okay?—or the waste disposal pick-up, which is handled the safest way possible for everyone—it's just about being with a family who loves you for as long as you're on this earth." She stared out into the audience, forcing them to hear what she couldn't say aloud.

"Then we go to heaven," Singha said in a clear, bell-like voice. "Don't forget the heaven part, Janis."

"Thank you, Singha," she said hoarsely. "Yeah, then we go to heaven. Thanks for your time, everybody." She glanced at her mother and nearly burst out bawling at the mixture of sadness and pride in her eyes.

"Will you really take down the sign?" the rude man said, planting his hands on his hips and glaring at them.

Zoe's started. "What? Oh, certainly. I said we'd be more than willing to compromise—"

"Well, then, I don't see what all this fuss is about," he said, scowling. "You take down the sign, we'll call it even."

"Uh . . . what about the waste disposal truck?" Zoe stammered.

The man made an impatient gesture. "What about it? Like you said, it's the best way to get rid of the stuff, so what the hey?" He turned to the rest of the audience.

174

"Come on people, take a vote. Are you ready to go home or what?"

Janis watched, hardly daring to believe as the crowd rose and gathered their things. Several of the women approached them and under the guise of apologizing, reached out and tentatively stroked the top of Jeffrey or Gabriel or Singha's heads. Hope had suckered herself to Janis and wouldn't let herself be touched.

"And you, missy," the rude man said, stopping in front of Janis and gazing at her with a gimlet eye. "When the weather warms up, you bring this group down to the house on the corner. I know the cranky old codger who lives there and he always keeps his freezer stocked with ice cream sandwiches. Got that?"

"Okay," Janis said, blinking.

He glanced down at Hope and his face creased into a smile, then he turned and stomped out.

"I have to sit down," Janis muttered.

"How did counseling go?" Cassandra asked as Faizon climbed into the BMW. She pulled away from the hospital, pretending not to realize she hadn't given him a hello kiss and joined the flow of traffic heading back into Chandler. Her whole body felt heavy and it was taking a serious effort to keep her voice light and her expression calm and unconcerned.

"Okay," he said slowly. "Is everything all right, Cass?"

"Sure," she said, forcing a smile. "As a matter of fact, we've been invited skiing next weekend at the Parrish's cabin. What do you think?" Because I think if I don't get my period soon I'm going to throw myself off of the nearest cliff, she thought, gripping the steering wheel.

"It's a great invitation but I have to tell you, I don't know how to ski," he said, sounding embarrassed. "It's an expensive sport and I've never had enough money to—"

Pay for an abortion? she substituted silently. Support an instant family? "Don't worry, Faizon. We have extra gear and if you want to learn to ski, I can teach you. Natalie doesn't know how either but she doesn't want to learn."

"Then, great, I won't be the only non-skier. Sure, I'd like to go." He shifted closer and wrapping one of his hands gently around hers, pried it from the steering wheel. "Sorry but it's hard for me to sit here without touching you." He brushed his lips across her temple. "You sure you're okay?"

"Fine," she said, keeping her eyes on the road so he wouldn't see the fear inside her. She didn't want to deal with this, she wanted to go back to the way it had been before they'd made love. "So, where do you want to go?"

"Well, that's a hard one," he said, smiling. "My place is out. We could go to your house."

"No," she said, shaking her head. "Everybody's home and I don't feel like dealing with them. And besides, my parents don't know the ski trip's gonna be co-ed and if you slip up and tell them, we won't be able to go."

"I don't like to lie, Cassandra," he said, frowning.

"You don't have to lie, just don't volunteer anything," she said impatiently and then stopped, shocked. "I sound just like Natalie."

He laughed. "Is that as bad as you make it sound?"

"If you knew Nat, you wouldn't even have to ask,"

she said grimly, pulling up in front of the Green Café. "Since there's really nowhere else for us to go, want to get something to eat?"

"We could go out to the park," he murmured, pressing his mouth to her ear. "Cass, I'd love to hold you again. I don't mean like that," he said, drawing back when she stiffened. "I just want to be alone with you."

"But not like that?" she said, meeting his dark gaze. She wanted to be alone with him, too, but she didn't want to feel like every time they were alone they were supposed to make love.

"Cass," he said solemnly. "What we did the other day . . . that was a mutual thing, we both wanted to. That's the only way it's ever gonna happen with us and I don't want you to think any different. I love you, you know."

She took a deep breath and some of the tension slipped away. "Let's get a couple of take-out coffees then and go up to the park. Faizon?" She touched his arm. "I love you, too."

"And that's how I found out you were . . . uh, gay," Stephanie said, blotting her mouth with a napkin and avoiding her father's gaze. It was weird; the gay part of this whole thing had taken a backseat to everything else and she'd only told him the story about her mother and Mr. Earl to explain why she'd never answered any of his letters.

"And how do you feel about that?" he said, watching her.

She shrugged. "I haven't really thought about it much. I was so freaked at finally finding out where you were and how Mom had lied that everything else just sort of got pushed aside. And to be totally honest with you, you're my father and I can't imagine you messing around with *anybody,* if you know what I mean, so I'm not even thinking about it." Blushing, she stared down at her plate. "But aren't you scared of AIDS, Dad?"

"Of course I am and if you're sexually active, you should be too," he said. "Ron and I have been together in a monogamous relationship for seven years now. We're completely committed to each other and we both get tested annually because the virus *does* take so long to surface. So put your mind at ease as far as I'm concerned, Stephanie, and promise me that if you're going to be with someone, you'll always use a condom."

"Okay," she mumbled. "Can we change the subject now?"

"Sure," he said, sounding amused. "Would you like me to tell you about your bank account?"

Her head shot up. "My *what?*"

"Really Stephanie, you didn't think just because your mother refused my child support payments that I'd take them back, did you?" he said, eyes twinkling. "No, no, no. Each of my daughters has a bank account in her name—"

"Oh, my God," Stephanie said.

"—with nearly eight years of payments deposited—"
Her jaw dropped.

"—with a separate portion to be used for college—"
– She didn't have to rely on a scholarship.

"—and a percentage to remain as savings but the rest is to be used in your daily life."

I can quit biology now, she thought, staring at him. I can quit biology and cut my work hours and . . . and . . .

"I want to buy some clothes," she said. "And I want to take some more writing classes. Can I do that?"

"Be my guest," he said, smiling.

She rose, walked around the table and put her arms around him. "Thank you," she whispered.

Fourteen

"Did you remember to bring a chain?" Janis asked on Monday morning, meeting Maria in the parking lot. They huddled by the gym's back entrance, seeking protection from the relentless wind.

"This is the only one I could find," Maria said, hoisting the brown bag. "The padlock's kind of flimsy."

"Hmmm," Janis said, examining it. "Mine's heavier, you'd better use that one. We don't want him escaping before he sees the error of his ways, right?"

"I guess," Maria said weakly. Friday's outrage had faded and now the thought of chaining herself to Coach Garry wasn't a such a hot one. What if he had them suspended? Or expelled?

"You still want to do it, don't you?" Janis said, tucking her hair behind her ear and revealing a row of NOW earrings.

"Do you?" Maria countered, hoping she said no.

"Look, he dissed you big time in front of all those guys and then he blew you off when you tried explaining how embarrassing it was so, yeah, I do," Janis said.

"What if he's sorry?" Maria said, squirming. "I mean, what if we walk in there now and he's real nice to us?"

Janis held up a hand. "Tell you what; we'll go in but I won't do one thing until you say . . . uh . . ."

"Phase Two," Maria said. "If I say that, then we chain ourselves to him. If I don't, then we leave, okay?"

"It's your call," Janis said, sighing.

Why does this place always smell like the bottom of a hamper, Janis wondered, wrinkling her nose and following Maria into the noisy gym. A herd of guys were running laps and as soon as they spotted Maria, the whistling and leering started.

"Coach Garry's by the stage," Maria said. "And remember, if I don't say—"

"I'm way ahead of you," Janis said, reaching deep into the pocket of her father's old olive drab trench coat and fingering the padlock attached to the chain. She felt bad for Maria because she knew they'd end up chained to the sexist coach. There was no way this guy was gonna apologize without a serious talking to.

"Hey, there she is," Coach Garry bellowed, spotting Maria. "I told you guys she'd be back for more. Hey, Torres, jog on over here and inspire us."

Maria blushed as a chorus of catcalls echoed through the gym and tight-lipped, she muttered, "Oh, crap. Phase Two."

That's all I wanted to hear, Janis thought, loping to the far side of Coach Garry and pretending to be searching her pockets for something. The trench coat was huge, hanging nearly to the floor and she'd worn it for more than its sacklike pockets. It made her look like a little

181

kid playing dress-up which was perfect because she wanted to look as unthreatening as possible until the deal went down.

"Torres, if you've got such a problem with us big, hairy brutes, why're you back in here, flashing your—"

If he says hooters, I'm gonna poke him right in the eye, Janis thought, scowling.

"—self around in front of my team?" He glanced at Janis and dismissed her without a second thought.

"This is my school and I should be able to walk around without being harassed," Maria said, growing very red. "And without having that harassment condoned by the teachers!"

Nice touch, Janis thought, readying her chain. She'd told Maria she'd go for his ankle first, mostly as a distraction so Maria could slip her loop around his wrist.

"Look Torres, my job is to bond with these fellas—"

Here goes nothing, Janis thought, crouching and nearly disappearing into the enormous trenchcoat. Deftly, she pulled the chain from her pocket, looped it around his ankle and had begun drawing it tight when the coach noticed what she was doing.

"What the hell?" he blurted, yanking his leg away.

"Oh, no you don't," Janis said, lunging after the chain. She snagged it and swung her leg around, fumbling with the padlock.

"Got him," Maria cried triumphantly.

"Me, too," Janis said, panting as she snapped the padlock shut around her own ankle. Man, that had been too close to call.

"Look, I know you girls like me, but isn't this going a little too far?" He looked from Maria to Janis, who lay sprawled out on the floor. "And who's she, anyway? Mata Hari?"

"You wish," Janis said. "What I am, at this point, is one hundred and fifteen pounds of dead weight shackled to your ankle, Coach Garry, and I'm going to stay that way until we talk about your dissing the girls in this place." She lifted her head, grinned and lying, said, "Whoa, nice underwear, Coach. A little frayed around the edges but hey, it just—"

Swearing, he clamped down the legs of his gym trunks, dragging one of Maria's arms with him, which seemed to drive home the fact that he was now in a serious dilemma. "All right, you girls have had your joke. Now get out before the bell rings."

"He still doesn't get it," Janis said, heaving a sigh.

"This isn't a joke, Coach," Maria said quietly.

The joggers gathered around, gaping. "What're you looking at?" Coach Garry snapped, steaming. "Hit the showers. *Now.*"

Janis folded her hands behind her head and winked at Brian, who looked like he wanted to murder her. "Shake it, baby," she drawled, laughing as he wheeled and strode away.

The last guy disappeared into the locker room.

"Now," Coach Garry barked, turning on Maria. "Are you gonna tell me what's going on here or do I have to call the principal?"

Maria flinched but stood her ground. "I was serious when I said you embarrassed me but you didn't care. I couldn't even cut through the gym without hearing a bunch of gross comments from not only the guys but from *you.*"

"What did I say?" he blustered, turning red.

Janis lifted her head. "Allow me," she said and rattled off every sexist comment he'd made. "Really, Coach. You know as well as we do how far over the line you went. 'A handful of that? Greyhounds chasing a rabbit?' What kind of comments are those for a teacher to make about a student in front of a bunch of other students? If a regular teacher had said those things, he'd be brought before the school board and the PTA and I'm sure he'd—"

"So what is this, blackmail?" he interrupted, scowling.

"No," Maria said, keeping an eye on the freshly showered guys straggling out into the main hallway, where a crowd seemed to be gathering. "All I want is for you to act like a teacher. Stop going into the girls' locker room—"

He stiffened. "Now wait a minute, here."

"Every girl on that cheerleading squad has had to lockerdive because of you," Maria said angrily. "Your job is to be a role model, Coach, not one of the guys. We have feelings, too and maybe we don't think our bodies should be commented on, okay?"

"Fine," he said, avoiding her gaze. "You done now?"

"Are you?" Janis said, propping her head on her hand. "C'mon Coach, you didn't like it when I looked up your shorts and made a judgment call; what if I'd done it in front of a bunch of girls? Or what if there are guys out there dissing your daughter the same way you dissed Maria and the only guy that could've saved her acted even worse?" She sat up and unlocked her padlock.

Maria hesitated. "We only did this because you wouldn't have listened otherwise. D'you understand?"

"Sure, I understand," he said in an ominously calm voice. "Now, would you mind getting off my arm before the bell rings?"

"We're not gonna say anything," Maria began.

"As long as you remember that girls are human beings and should be treated with respect," Janis added, rising and stowing her chain back in her trench coat pocket. "Ready, Maria?"

"Yeah," Maria said, unlocking herself.

The coach jerked free and strode into his office.

"Think that accomplished anything?" Maria said, flinching as the slamming door echoed through the gym.

"Too soon to tell," Janis said. Man, she had a bad feeling about this. "C'mon, he'll only get madder if he has to look at us." She snorted, dismissing her unease as a case of post-protest jitters. "Isn't that a shame. Looking's what got him into this mess in the first place."

"What is it with you, Torres?" Vanessa sneered, cornering her in the hall after class.

"What're you talking about?" Maria said, but she already knew. The guys from practice must have been spreading the word because she'd been getting more than her share of dirty looks lately.

"What do you have against Coach Garry now?"

"What makes you think I have something against him?" Maria said, trying to brazen her way through. "Don't listen to the grapevine, Vanessa. You know how people exaggerate."

"Not when it comes to you," Vanessa said. "What're you, some kind of guy-hater all of a sudden?"

Maria stood there, speechless.

Was that what people really thought?

"I can't believe you did that," Brian said, shooting

Janis an incredulous look across the Bronco. "I mean, you humiliated the guy in front of the whole team—"

"That wasn't our intent," Janis said. Well, maybe a little.

"But that's what happened," he snapped, running a hand through his hair. "Man, of all the stupid things to do—"

Janis's temper slipped. "You weren't this freaked when he humiliated Maria. Why, because waving your crotches at girls is considered good clean fun in the jock world? Spare me."

"Nobody waved their crotch at Maria," he said.

"No, they just offered to be human bras and your beloved coach egged them on and you know it, so don't get down on me because we decided to fight back."

"Okay, well if you don't give a crap about Coach Garry, what about me, Jan? Most of those guys are my friends—"

"Then maybe you need some new friends," Janis said.

He stared at her for a moment. "Forget it, just forget it. You're not gonna hear anything you don't want to hear." He opened the door and slid out. "I'll tell you something, Janis. If I ever embarrassed you in front of your friends the way you just did to me, you'd never talk to me again. Think about *that.*"

"I would so," she said, scowling as he walked away.

186

Fifteen

It was, all things considered, a horrible week.

The Coach Garry-incident rumbled through the student body like an ongoing tremor and the tide of disgust against Janis and Maria increased. No one knew the truth and by the time Maria was finally upset enough to speak out, no one cared. Coach Garry, in spite of his sexist attitude, had been a favorite and the senior guys went out of their way to make sure Maria knew it. Janis, who'd spent most of her high school life being sneered at by the jock clique didn't seem to care but Maria, who'd hung with them, gone to their houses and their parties, couldn't believe how much they seemed to hate her now.

"I only stood up for myself," she said at the lunch table. "Why do I have to be the bad guy in this?"

"Don't worry about it," Janis said, sighing. "The whole thing'll die down sooner or later. Any time you buck the system, somebody's gonna freak, okay?"

"But the whole school hates us," Maria said miserably. "Even the janitor gave me a dirty look the other day."

"I'll trade you," Simon drawled, sauntering up. "Your dirty look for my black eye." He grinned into their shocked faces. "Think I'm gonna have to cut gym for a while."

"Somebody hit you?" Maria cried, covering her mouth and staring at the reddish-purple bruise beneath his eye. "Oh, no."

"Hey, the locker room's a dangerous place these days," he said, slipping into the seat next to Maria. "No big deal. Brian jumped in before they did any serious damage."

"Brian helped you?" Janis asked.

Simon laughed. "Yeah, and now he's wearing the other half of these psychedelic glasses," he said, touching the black eye.

"Think I should go find him?" Janis asked uneasily.

"I think he's gonna find you," Simon said, crunching into a pretzel rod. "Man, revolution really gives me an appetite."

Cassandra collapsed across her bed. She was dripping sweat, panting, and her leg muscles were rubbery with exhaustion. She'd been dancing like a fiend all week, exercising, praying, anything to bring on the one period that would give her a second chance.

There were signs it *could* be coming but according to Natalie, who had evolved into some sort of mid-wife/doom-sayer, tender breasts and bloating were also signs of pregnancy.

The tape clicked onto the flip side.

Cassandra struggled up and padded tiredly back to the studio. She had some serious dancing to do.

* * *

"Mom, it's perfectly good money," Stephanie said, trying to force a wad of bills into her mother's hands. "Dad's been putting it aside for almost eight years. Will you take it, already?"

"We don't need his guilt money," Mrs. Ling said stiffly.

"Yes, we do," Stephanie snapped, whipping it down onto the kitchen table. "Things are gonna change around here, Mom. I've cut my hours down at the Green Café—"

Mrs. Ling's head jerked. "What?"

"And I'm gonna buy some new clothes and have some fun for a while," Stephanie continued defiantly. "I don't mind helping but I'm not gonna be the Dad to your Mom any more. We have a father and if you don't want to tell the girls yet that he's gay, that's your decision but you should let them see him. He's not a monster, he's our father and we have a right to get to know him again."

Mrs. Ling went to the sink and turned on the water, drowning out the echo of Stephanie's words.

Natalie was upstairs on Hope's bed, reading aloud and wondering if Hope, who was playing across the room, was even listening, when she heard the front door open.

"Delivery," someone called cheerfully.

Natalie froze. The book hit the floor with a thump.

"Oh, how beautiful," one of the volunteers exclaimed. "I didn't know the daffodils were blooming already."

"Hey, for Harmony House, no problem," Edan said. "I've got fresh daisies for the kids' rooms, too. Mind if I go on up?"

Oh, no, Natalie thought, heart pounding. She didn't

know what to do or where to go, or worse, what to say when he—

"Natalie." He stopped in the doorway, surprised.

"Hi," she croaked, swallowing hard. "Nice flowers."

He glanced down at the daisies as if just remembering they were there. "Yeah, huh? Hey there, Hope." He crossed the room, smiling past Natalie at the little girl but the color staining his cheeks belied his casual movements. "So Nat, ready to go skiing?"

"Yeah. You?"

"Sure. The worst part's getting up so early to leave." He plucked the old daisies from the vase and dropped them into the garbage. "You guys got the caravan figured out?"

"Um, yeah." She racked her brain, trying to remember the driving arrangements. "Janis is driving, Joey's driving, and I'm going with your sister. You're bringing your van, right?"

"It'll be loaded full of supplies." His back was to her and his voice was light but this was the second daisy stem he'd snapped and set aside. "Done." He gathered the remaining flowers and headed for the door. "Bye, Hope. See you tomorrow, Natalie."

"See you." She picked up the book and resumed reading.

Sixteen

"Man, are you devious," Cassandra murmured, eyeing Natalie.

"I have no idea what you're talking about," she said, smirking and tossing her cousin a duffle bag. They were loading Janis's Bronco and the crisp air crackled with anticipation.

"Having Janis pick up all the girls before we go get Faizon, Simon, and Brian?" Cassandra said with a pointed look. "C'mon Nat, that move has your name written all over it."

"Hey, if you can't beat 'em, go around 'em," Natalie said, shrugging. "I mean, this is a perfectly legit trip but your parents would've freaked if they knew there were guys going along, so . . . why tell them?"

You make it sound so easy, Cassandra thought, glancing back at the porch where her parents were handing Janis a bakery box to pass on to the Parrishes as a thank-you.

"Well, that's the last of it," Natalie said. "Let's go say goodbye. Oh . . . hey Cass, anything on you-know-what yet?"

"Nothing," she said and suddenly, the sun seemed dimmer.

The Parrish's driveway was a madhouse. The baggage was being packed, Janis was bounding around like a hyperactive gazelle, unable to speak in anything less than a bellow and Jesse and Edan looked like they wanted to throttle her. Mr. Parrish was a weathered, preoccupied man who looked vaguely surprised every time he noticed the kids milling around his property and Mrs. Parrish, a tall, unflappable woman, had finished packing her own vehicle and was waiting patiently for the rest of them.

"Joey, Steph, Cass, and Faizon are going in Joey's Blazer," Janis hollered, waving them towards it. "Natalie, you're with Cleo. Brian, Simon, and Maria, you come with me."

"Behold our fearless leader," Simon said, smirking.

"And don't dawdle," she added, climbing into the driver's seat and starting the Bronco. "We're burning daylight."

"That girl is just begging to get beaned with a snowball," Brian muttered, making sure he had his gloves.

"Dissension in the ranks and we haven't even left yet," Simon said to Maria in a low, amused voice. "This is gonna be an interesting weekend."

Mr. and Mrs. Parrish led the caravan toward Snoqualmie National Forest, followed by Joey, then Janis (who had a terrible habit of taking her foot off the gas whenever she was talking, which meant the Bronco chugged on in a series of fits and starts, slowing to a

192

crawl then surging forward with a burst of warp speed that pinned its inhabitants against their seats), followed by a tormented Edan, with Cleo bringing up the rear.

"Man, we really are going into the wilderness," Natalie said uneasily, making sure her seatbelt was latched. The road had been growing progressively narrower and the snowdrifts higher, which amazed her as there hadn't been any snow at all back in Chandler. "Does this cabin of yours have electricity and stuff?"

"It has a generator but there's no phone or TV," Cleo said, lips twitching. "And yeah, it has indoor toilets. We'll have to turn the water on when we get there, though. The system shuts down when we leave so the pipes don't freeze."

"No TV," Natalie repeated, amazed. "I don't think I've ever been *anywhere* where there's no TV. Is there, like, a fireplace? Where are we gonna sleep?" What she really meant was "Where's Edan gonna sleep?" but that was a little too tacky for even her to ask his sister. And besides, if she *thought* it hard enough, Cleo would probably get a vibe or something and answer it anyway.

"Yeah, there's a fireplace," Cleo said and it sounded like she was trying hard not to laugh. "See, it's a log cabin so the kitchen and the main room is one big, open space. That's probably where the guys'll sleep."

"In the main room?"

"There are only two bedrooms, Nat. We'll be in the one off the kitchen and my parents'll take the upstairs loft."

Natalie narrowed her eyes, thinking furiously. If we had the loft, we could hang over the railing and bug them or even—

"Forget it," Cleo said, following Edan's van into a

snowy gravel parking lot. "My parents have already decided we get the bedroom. Sorry. Now, do you have to make a pitstop?"

"What?" Natalie said, bewildered.

"This is the general store, last chance for food, lodgings, and bathrooms before we head out to the cabin."

"How far out is this place, anyway?" Natalie said, worrying in earnest now. She was a city kid and all these huge, empty mountains were making her nervous.

"As the crow flies, over that ridge and across the meadow," Cleo said, pointing toward a vast expanse of snow. "As the road winds, it's a little longer." She glanced out the windshield and her eyebrows rose. "Ho, what do we have here? Snow bunnies?"

Two slim, pretty girls sporting neon ski gear and sipping Evian lounged across the store's railing, eyeing Edan and Jesse, who had gotten out of the van and were checking the roof rack.

"You know," Cleo mused, "I feel the need for a pack of gum."

"Me, too," Natalie said, opening the door. The frigid air hurt her teeth and froze her nostrils but she didn't care. She hadn't tracked Edan this far only to lose him to a snow rabbit.

"Bunny," Cleo said, snickering. "Snow *bunny.*"

"Whatever," Natalie said, returning her grin. She was getting used to Cleo's invisible antennae and wished she had the same ability to read people's auras or whatever they were. Then she would know how to get to Edan.

Cleo knelt near the railing to tie her shoelace and Natalie nearly fell over her. *Listen,* Cleo mouthed urgently.

"I'm telling you, that's the lead singer and the guitarist

194

from Corrupting Cleo," the taller girl said to her friend, eyeing the guys at the van. "I'd recognize them anywhere."

"I don't think you're right," the other girl said, frowning.

"Yeah, I am," she said. "Man, this is too intense. I've wanted to meet them for, like, a year. Listen, let's go over and ask them if they're from the band. Which one do you want?"

"I'll take the one with the black hair," the shorter girl said, sliding off the railing.

"Good, I like the other one better," the tall girl said, pulling on her thick, fur mittens. "Let's go for it." She passed Natalie with barely a glance.

"Do something," Natalie demanded, glaring at Cleo.

"What can I do?" she said. "I'm not 'Bewitched,' you know."

"Go spy on them," Natalie said impatiently. "I'll get the gum, you eavesdrop. Be Edan's pesky little sister . . . hey, if you really want to break it up, tell Janis you just heard those girls asking where the best place to trap . . . um, fox is around here."

"Wow, you're good," Cleo said admiringly and took off.

The general store was crowded and it took Natalie longer than she'd expected to get back outside. When she did, the girls were gone, Janis looked mutinous and Jesse and Edan were sitting in the van with the windows up and the motor running.

"Here she is," Cleo called, eyes sparkling. "We can go now." She hustled Natalie into the Jeep and burst out laughing.

"What happened?" Natalie asked, buckling her seat-belt.

"You mean you didn't hear? Those girls were asking where our cabin is when Janis stormed up and demanded to know who the slayer of innocent animals was. And then she spotted that girl's fur mittens and by the time she was through explaining, in gory detail, how many animals had been killed to make them, the girl was so mad she left." She shot Natalie a sideways glance as they followed the van back onto the road. "Nice job, Nat. Did you learn how to do that back in L. A.?"

"Yeah," Natalie said. "You've got to fight for every inch you get back in South Central. Nothing comes free."

The road to the cabin was a narrow, winding one. Janis had, at her passengers' pending mutiny, surrendered the wheel to Brian and was now glad. They'd skidded dangerously close to the edge of the embankment twice and she knew that if she'd been driving, she would've just covered her eyes and said her goodbyes.

"Hey, Jan, did you hear the latest on Coach Garry?" Simon drawled from the backseat.

"Do we have to talk about this now?" she said, watching as Brian's fingers tightened on the wheel. "If I'm gonna die I'd like it to be without having him on my mind." And besides, Coach Garry was still a very sore subject between her and Brian.

"What about Coach Garry?" Brian asked, glancing at Simon.

"He's transferring out of Seven Pines," Simon said, giving Janis an evil smirk. "This'll be his last year with us."

196

"What?" Brian yelped, slamming on the brakes as the Parrishes turned into a spacious clearing. "Where's he going?"

"St. Joe's," Simon said, gazing at the log cabin sitting smack in the middle of nowhere. "Hey, we're here, aren't we?"

"But St. Joe's is our biggest rival," Brian said in disbelief. "No. way."

"Yes way," Simon said, grinning.

"I think that's great," Janis said. "St. Joe's is an all boys' school, so now he'll have no one to harass. I think Maria and I did Seven Pines a favor, don't you?"

"Don't push it," Brian growled, throwing open his door and stepping out.

Janis turned and gave Simon a long, ominous look. "You'll pay for that, Pearlstein."

"Promises, promises," he said airily, then dodging Maria's playful punch, dove over the front seat and into the snow.

The cabin was freezing and while the Parrishes turned on the lights and water, the others went exploring.

"Wow, this place is gorgeous," Janis said, wide-eyed.

Cassandra shot her an incredulous look. Gorgeous? This cabin is as primitive as it can get and still be in this century, she thought, eyeing the fieldstone fireplace and huge wooden table flanked with picnic benches. The furniture was a conglomeration of pieces her mother would've burned before she'd even put out to the road and the only way to get to the loft was a set of steep, narrow steps behind the massive woodstove.

"I get a top bunk!" Janis shouted and was immediately echoed by Natalie's, "Me, too!"

Cassandra glanced at Stephanie. "They're already having a blast. Come on, let's go see our bedroom."

The bedroom wasn't really big enough for six girls and their gear. There were two sets of bunk beds, one double bed and an ancient, squatty bureau. The beds sported thick, down comforters which Janis wanted to boycott until Cleo said that if she didn't use it she'd freeze because there wasn't anything else.

Now I'm almost glad I *don't* have my period, Cassandra thought. There's no privacy at all and the only way to get to the bathroom is right through the middle of the main room. That ought to make showering a treat. I hardly know these people and now I'm going to have to live with them for two whole days.

She knelt next to her neatly packed bag and pretended to rummage through it so no one would see the tears in her eyes. I could be home right now, sleeping in my own bed in my own room without worrying about how fourteen people are gonna share a bathroom smaller than my closet. Whatever made me want to come?

Maria giggled.

Cassandra glanced up, spotting Brian in the bedroom doorway. Grinning, he put a finger to his lips, tiptoed across the noisy room and grabbing Janis, jammed a handful of snow down her back.

"Yeeeoo!" she screeched, sprawling across the duffle bags.

"Nyah nyah," he said, sticking his tongue out at her.

"Take it outside," Cleo called as Janis bolted after him.

Everyone else followed too, scrambling for gloves and hats, running and falling and screaming with laughter, bombarding each other with snowballs and crafty, sneak attacks engineered by Janis, who pretended to get hit in the eye and cry. When the guys came over to check her out, they were blasted backwards by a team of Valkyries fiercer than any Norsemen had ever dealt with.

Cassandra, gasping with laughter as Faizon caught one in the back of the head, stumbled over and fell to her knees beside him. She was soaked and tired and exhilarated, all at the same time. "Are you okay?" she said, helping him up and bending back down to retrieve his snow-filled cap.

"I'm fine," he said in a low voice, putting a hand on her arm and staying her. "But you're . . . uh, you're bleeding, Cassandra. The back of your pants are . . . uh . . ." He moved behind her, blocking the sight from the others. "What should I do?"

Cassandra stared at him, digesting his words and then a tiny flicker of hope began to glow deep in the pit of her stomach. She should have been embarrassed but if this was really her period, she wouldn't care. "Wait. Natalie?" she called. "Come here for a minute, will you?"

"No way," Natalie said, laughing. "Somebody'll nail me."

"Natalie," Cassandra repeated, trying not to sound like she was ready to explode.

"Oh, all right," Natalie said and staying low to avoid the snowballs, raced across the sidelines to Cassandra. "What?"

"I might have it." Cassandra held her gaze, watching as realization dawned in her cousin's eyes. "I'm gonna walk back to the cabin in front of you. You tell me what you think."

"Is everything okay?" Faizon asked.

"We'll let you know," Natalie said, brushing past him.

Please God, Cassandra prayed, heading back to the house. Don't let me have cut myself shaving my legs or anything stupid like that. "What do you think?"

"I think you'd better go into the bathroom and find out for sure," Natalie said slowly. "Did you bring tampons with you?"

"A brand new box. I was hoping they would inspire me." Her voice cracked. "Oh, Nat, if this isn't it—"

"Go," she said, shoving her through the door. "I'll wait."

Cassandra hurried to the bedroom, grabbed her purse and ran to the tiny, primitive bathroom. No flushing anything down this toilet, she thought, fumbling with her pants' zipper. She hesitated a moment, then took a deep breath and looked down.

She sat down and hands trembling, unwrapped the box of tampons.

"Cass?" Natalie called nervously, rapping on the door.

"I'm fine." The joy in her voice said it all.

"Are you sure you don't want to go skiing with the rest of them?" Stephanie asked Joey, feeling strangely shy. She usually saw him at night, under the cover of darkness or indoor lighting and the cold, icy sunshine exposed every inch of their faces like a magnifying glass. They were trudging through the snow along the woods with only their footsteps and their breathing breaking the silence. "I mean, you came up here to ski—"

"I'll ski tomorrow," he said, wrapping his arm around her. "I don't want to leave you the first day we're here.

It's not like I have so much time with you that I can throw it away."

She glanced up into his soft, brown eyes. He was, without a doubt, the nicest guy she'd ever met. "You're too much."

"Nah, just enough," he said, rubbing his cheek against her hair. "I could stay like this forever, just you and me and—"

"Yeah I know, six screaming kids," she said, laughing. "You really are funny, Joey. I mean, you don't even know me—"

"I know enough," he said seriously, kissing her. His mouth was warm and cold at the same time and it urged her closer. "Marry me, Steph and we'll honeymoon up here."

"Right," she murmured, smiling.

"I'm serious and you're laughing," he said, sounding hurt. "What do you think, I go around proposing to girls all the time? I want to marry you, Steph."

She stared at him, more than a little off balance. They'd just started going out. How could he make a lifelong commitment based on dating behavior? "And then what, we'll come home and move into the empty room in my mother's house?"

"Sure, until we can get a place of our own, why not?"

"And you'll go to work everyday while I finish high school?"

"You don't have to finish school, Steph. I didn't. My father needed me in the business and it's good money, so I quit. You can quit and work full-time if you want."

She took a step backwards. "But then what about my college?"

"Do you really think you need it?" he said, making a face. "I mean, you seem like a pretty smart girl to me."

"Joey." She placed her hand on his chest, wondering if the thunder she felt was his heart or her own pulse reflecting back to her. "This is going way too fast for me. I mean, I'm glad we're seeing each other and all but . . . well, I just found out I don't have to work like a dog anymore and you know what? I don't *want* to. I want to hang with you and my friends, take writing classes and yeah, I want to go to college."

He watched her, silent.

"And since I'm on a roll," she said with a weak smile, "I might as well tell you that I'm not even sure I want kids. I practically raised my sisters and I know how hard it is. I don't know if I want to do it again. You're freaked now, I can tell."

"You're right," he said gruffly, shaking his head as if to clear it. "Man, Steph, you sure know how to pack a wallop."

"I'm not what you thought I was," she said.

"Not exactly."

"That's okay because I'm not what *I* thought I was either," she said, taking his slack hand and squeezing it. "So, do you still like me or do you want to move on? You can tell me, you won't hurt my feelings." She caught his look and flushed. "Well, maybe a little but I swear I won't hold it against you. If you're looking to get married—"

"Steph." Smiling, he put a hand over her mouth. "Hang on a minute, would you? I wasn't looking to get married, I was looking to marry *you*. There's a difference you know. Now that you said marriage was out . . ." He shrugged.

She pulled his hand away. "Go on."

"What can I say? We'll just shack up once you get out of college," he said, laughing. "Man, is my old man gonna have a fit." He bumped his shoulder against hers. "Anything else you want to blow me away with, kid?"

"Well, now that you mention it," she said slowly, glancing up at him. "Did I ever tell you why my parents divorced?"

"I'll make you a deal," he said, eyes twinkling. "You tell me about your parents and I'll tell you about the time Blind Vito tried to shave off Angelina's moustache while she was sleeping but missed and got her eyebrow instead—"

She kissed him. "My father left my mother because he's gay."

"Your mother got a moustache?" he teased.

"No!"

"Well, tell her to grow one and maybe he'll come back." Laughing, he took off across the meadow.

Grinning, Stephanie ran after him.

Look at me, Edan, Natalie thought, bombarding his brain with her request. Look up from your dinner plate and into my eyeballs.

Edan chewed his hamburger and talked to Jesse.

I should've sat across from him, Natalie thought. Sure, I would've ended up kicking him under the table but it still would have been better than this. Today he went out skiing and tomorrow he's gonna go out skiing and then we're gonna leave and I'm not gonna be any better off than I was before.

She snorted, earning a curious look from Cassandra,

who was sitting next to her and holding Faizon's hand under the table.

"You okay?" Cassandra murmured.

"Oh, sure, I'm great," Natalie said, glowering.

"Hey kid, how about spelling me?" Jesse said, whacking his sister across the butt with the damp dishtowel.

"No way," Maria said, smirking. "Watching you be domestic is way too entertaining. Heck, I wish I'd brought a camera."

"I did," Janis piped up from the sink, where she was elbow-deep in dishwater. "Why don't you get it and take some pictures?"

"Thanks a lot," Jesse said, giving Janis, who he hadn't forgiven for ragging on those two girls earlier, a dirty look.

"No problem," she said, beaming at him. "Don't you think this is fun, Jesse? Just the fourteen of us up here in the mountains, braving the elements, bonding together—"

—committing mass murder, he finished silently.

"Be nice," Cleo murmured, loitering at his side.

"I wasn't gonna say it," he said, before he realized there was no way she could have known what he was thinking. And then he realized she hadn't been on the slopes today but tomorrow she'd probably come with them and then he'd have to explain how bad he felt about causing her accident before she told him how much she hated him because once those words left her mouth, he'd never be able to look at her again.

"Say cheese," Maria said, going on a picture-snapping spree.

"Jesse," Cleo said softly. "I think we'd better talk."

Her hair was grazing his arm, lingering on his skin like a spiderweb but he had no urge to brush it away. Her wide, amber eyes seemed to draw him down until the room faded and the only thing focused was her face. So this is what it feels like, he mused. Nobody ever tells you it's like having tunnel vision.

"Jesse?" Janis nudged him. "Here's the next plate to dry."

"Oh, great," he said, grabbing it. He felt weird, like the earth had tilted and he was struggling to remain upright. He glanced down at the dishcloth then across the room to where Cleo was breaking up kindling for the fireplace. Had she actually been here with him or had he imagined the whole thing?

An idea struck and before he could dismiss it as stupid, he took a deep breath and shouted silently, *Cleo.*

She jerked and the branch she was holding fell to the floor.

He turned away before she could do something unnerving like lift her head, meet his gaze and say, "What?"

You're really losing it, Jess, he told himself. You're so freaked at being back up here that the next thing you'll be doing is writing some kind of mystical ode or . . .

Or finishing a ballad.

Natalie got stuck playing Songburst with everyone but Edan, who sat in the shadows, strumming his acoustic guitar and Jesse, who was hunched next to him, scribbling on a sheet of paper.

205

"I know that one," Janis cried, screeching out the lyrics to The Guess Who's "Share the Land."

Edan stiffened.

Jesse shuddered.

Natalie grinned, glad she wasn't the only one suffering.

"Hey, Simon," Maria said forlornly later that night, leaning against the porch railing and gazing up into the cloudy, starless sky. "Do you think we were wrong to do that to Coach Garry?"

"Bummed, huh?" he said, sliding his arm around her. "Hey, you had a right to defend yourself. Unfortunately, the Sandifer-Wayne troll didn't realize that you're used to playing by different rules. Janis likes being a social misfit; she gets off on stirring people up. I'm not saying she doesn't believe in her causes because she does; I'm just saying Janis's solution isn't always the one that works best for everybody." He grinned. "I admire her. She's whacked but she's got guts."

And I don't, Maria finished silently. "Did you ever go out with her?"

He shuddered. "I'd rather wear a dress to a Singles Dance in Leavenworth Prison than to get with the troll. No, we'll be buds forever but that's about as far as it goes. There are some lines you just don't cross."

"And going out with friends is one of them?" Maria said.

His mouth curved into a lazy grin. "Why do I get the feeling this is a loaded question?"

"Just answer it," Maria said, snaking a hand up beneath his jacket and tickling him. He leaned against the railing, watching her until finally, frustrated, she quit. "I

206

figures you wouldn't be ticklish," she said, shooting him a dark look.

"The next obvious question," he drawled, "is 'are you'?"

"No," she said too quickly and waited for him to find out.

He didn't. The night breeze stirred his hair and the gleam in his eyes deepened. "I should take your word for it, Scarlett because I hate the thought of screwing up a decent friendship." He lowered his mouth to her cheek, close but not touching her lips and when he spoke, the words were warm and shivery against her skin. "You don't want to screw it up either, do you?"

"Of course not," she said, only half meaning it.

"That's what I thought," he murmured, easing her closer. "You know what's great about being friends?"

"No," she said, relaxing against him.

"You can delude yourself into believing stuff like this is on the level," he said with a rueful smile. "Now, you'd better hit me with a snowball so I have a reason for being dazed and confused."

She did, splatting him square in the forehead and wishing she'd put a big, pointy rock inside it.

"Cass?" Natalie hung upside down off the top of her bunk and peered into the gloom at her cousin. "Are you asleep?"

"Yes," Cassandra murmured.

"I have to go to the bathroom," Natalie said.

"So go," Cleo said from the double bed she was sharing with Maria. "You know the way."

"Okay," Natalie said, scrambling down. That's all she'd

wanted to hear. She didn't really have to go and the thought of wasting all this time while Edan was just a room away was too much to bear. Not that I'm gonna do anything, she told herself, tugging down her knee-length T-shirt and reslouching her socks. All I want to do is reach him before we have to leave tomorrow.

"Nat?" Cleo said softly. "My parents are light sleepers."

"Gotcha," Natalie said, tiptoeing out into the main room. The fireplace glowed molten red and she hesitated, accustoming her eyes and trying to figure out which huddled mass was Edan.

That's all I need to do is proposition the wrong guy by mistake, she thought, grinning. That sounds like Joey snoring and the mumbler's gotta be Simon. There's Faizon, there's Jesse . . . *aha*. There's Edan, in the day bed. I can tell by all that great hair.

She padded swiftly across the room, leaned over to wake him up and found him watching her.

"Oh," she said, suddenly very aware of the fireplace's heat and her bare, winter legs and the fact that she was above him and he was below her and if she wanted to, she could slip under those covers faster than he could slip out.

"You've got the worst timing," he murmured, smiling.

"Shhh," she whispered, putting a hand over his mouth. "Listen, can I drive home with you tomorrow?"

He caught hold of her hand and keeping it tucked inside his own, settled it on his chest. "Why?"

There's some serious torture going down here, she thought, starting to sweat. His strong, calloused hand rubbed against her trapped one with every breath he took and if he didn't quit it and let her go, he was gonna need

208

reinforcements to peel her off him. "Because I want to talk to you." She pulled free. "So?"

"Okay," he said, nodding.

She blinked, surprised. "Fine. See you tomorrow."

"What'd he say?" Cleo mumbled when Natalie padded back into the bedroom.

"You're driving home with Jesse tomorrow," Natalie said, giving her a smug look and clambering back up into her bunk.

Now she could sleep.

Seventeen

"Bye," Janis called, waving to the skiers, then turned
to Stephanie and Natalie. "Want to build a snow
fort?"

"Why?" Natalie said, eyeing her amusedly.

"Because we're here and there's snow," Janis said, as
if it was obvious. "C'mon, we'll make the walls real high
and I'll even donate my red scarf as its banner. We'll call
it Fort—"

"Courage?" Stephanie suggested, giggling.

"I'm Sergeant O'Rourke," Natalie said, pulling her
gloves from her pockets. "C'mon Corporal Agarn, let's
go build the old man a fort to be proud of."

"What old man?" Janis asked, frowning.

"You, Cap'n," Natalie and Stephanie said together,
laughing.

Jesse watched as Cleo disappeared down the slope.
His teeth were chattering and his entire body numb but
not from the cold. This was the slope he'd challenged

her on three years ago and if he lived to be a hundred, he'd never forget that day or, it seemed, this one.

I have to go after her, he thought, shivering. If I don't do another right thing for the rest of my life, at least I'll have done this. Man, this is gonna be bad.

The sky was hung with clouds and the heavy, moisture-laden wind scraped his face. He was alone in the forbidding silence and suddenly the ballad he'd written trickled into his mind, dividing his fear into smaller, more manageable pieces.

She steps into the night,
completes the darkness
with her summer smile and eyes that
see past the parts of me
covered in other people's prints.

He took a deep breath and pushed off, steering neatly past the stand of leafless trees rushing up to meet him.

She celebrates rain
and walks with spirit laughter.
Her mouth knows the heat
of a battle untouched by
other people's prints.

The frigid air burned his skin and crept into his bones.

She carries the light
in hands that reach for nothing
and says there's music in your soul,
so let's move with it . . .

She dances through time and
greets the truth with
a summer smile and eyes that
see the best of me
untouched by other people's prints . . .

He crested the hill and there she was, standing beneath the ancient, towering pine tree. She waved, her red hair a bloodspot against the snow and his breath exploded in a harsh, ragged sound and it was only then he realized that it was all right, he wasn't going to find her here twice, crumpled and pale and near death.

"Took you long enough," she said when he skied up. "I was beginning to think you weren't coming to my reunion."

"I don't know how you can joke about this place," he said. "I don't even know how you can come back here, Cleo."

She gazed at him, then held out her hand. "Trust me?"

He looked at it and felt the bone-cold fear fade. "Okay," he said, letting her lead him to the tree. Its fresh, tangy scent enveloped him like an invisible bubble and when she knelt and touched the bark he did too, not knowing precisely why.

"This is where I hit," she said quietly. "There was one second of pain and then everything stopped."

Memories surged and his chest constricted, making him fight for breath. Time wavered and for a moment, three years ago was now and he was paralyzed with terror. He gripped her hand, waiting for the rescue team, calling on God and the angels and anyone else who could help because yeah, he'd known how to hurt her but he sure as hell hadn't known how to help.

212

"I was drifting, no pain, no nothing, just drifting like an astronaut with a cut line." She was looking through him, seeing something he couldn't. "When I found the tunnel, the light was more beautiful than anything I can ever describe."

"Cleo," he said hoarsely. "I'm really sorry—"

"No," she breathed, giving him a luminous smile. "No more. I don't want you to be sorry because *I'm* not sorry. When those women sent me back, they gave me a wonderful gift. They gave me peace in my soul." She pressed his hand to her glowing cheek. "Jesse, stop thinking something bad happened three years ago. I wouldn't trade what I am today for anything in the world."

He blinked, mesmerized by her radiant smile. She doesn't hate me, he thought. She doesn't blame me for ruining her life.

This was followed by a far more unsettling thought. But if she's nuts, she wouldn't think her life was screwed-up anyway.

"Stop worrying," Cleo said, meeting his astonished gaze. "I've never blamed you for what happened back then. C'mon." She rose, tugging him hurriedly out from under the tree.

"What's the matter?" he asked.

"Wait," she said softly.

Seconds later there was a sharp *crack* and a branch crashed to the ground where they'd been kneeling.

He froze. She couldn't have known that was going to happen, it was a coincidence, she must've heard it breaking before . . .

"Think what you want," she said amusedly. "We'd better leave now. There's a storm coming."

She was halfway down the hill before he'd recovered enough to follow.

"There's a blizzard coming," Mrs. Parrish said, greeting the skiers at the door. "We're going to have to leave immediately to make the main road before it hits. Let's pack and get loaded."

"Darn it, there goes our fort," Janis said, eyeing the magnificent structure. "Well, I'm gonna leave our banner there, anyway. Long live Fort Courage."

The wind surged and the group leaped into action. Duffle bags were hauled back out, sleeping bags rolled up and chaos ensued.

"I can't believe we spread out so fast in only a day and a half," Maria said, peering beneath the bed. "Whose socks?"

"If they're purple toe socks, they're mine," Janis said.

Things were even worse in the main room.

"I know I'm forgetting something," Edan said, running a hand through his hair and gazing around the frenzied room.

"You got your guitar?" Jesse asked, tucking his ballad into his back pocket and wondering if he should show it to Cleo on the ride home. There was no reason not to— she'd listened to their efforts before—but this time, well, he just didn't know.

"Yeah, it's by the front door."

"What about the food?" Maria called. "Can we leave it here?"

"No, pack it up and put it back in my van," Edan said, scowling. "Damn, what am I forgetting, Jess?"

"It's snowing," Natalie said, coming up beside them. "Hard."

By the time the trucks were loaded the snow was swirling and coating the ground with a rapidity that was frightening.

"Everything's off, Mom," Edan called, opening Natalie's door and motioning her into the van. "Heat, water, the whole nine yards. I locked up. Let's get moving." He climbed into the driver's side and followed Cleo's Jeep down the driveway. "I *know* I'm forgetting something but I can't figure out what."

Natalie watched nervously as the windshield wipers battled what seemed to be a never-parting curtain of snow. "Are we gonna make this all right, Edan?"

"Don't worry," he said, with a reassuring glance. "It's not that bad. As long as it stays this way till we can at least get to the general store, we'll be fine. We've driven home in worse."

"Are you sure you're not just saying that to make me feel better?" She touched her seatbelt, comforted by its tight fit.

He smiled. "Did it make you feel better?"

"Yeah," she admitted, grinning. "Lie to me some more."

The van lurched and Edan's smile died. "Let me concentrate on driving for a while first," he said, falling back to give Cleo's Jeep breathing room. The snow seemed to be decreasing slightly and up ahead, the caravan was making better time.

The lull lasted only minutes and the snow increased as the trucks eased down onto the narrow, one lane road.

"Does this thing have four wheel drive?" Natalie mumbled, clutching her door handle as they skidded. The road was covered and their only guides were the tree-lined embankments on either side.

"No, but we're carrying a lot of weight," Edan said quietly. "We'll be fine, Nat. I won't let anything happen to you. Look, here comes the general store—"

"What?" she asked, startled as he swore and hit the wheel.

"I know what I forgot," he said grimly, flashing his high beams at Cleo and following her into the parking lot. "My wallet fell out of my pocket while I was playing the guitar and I put it on the windowsill so I wouldn't lose it. I have to go back."

"Now?" Natalie said, stomach sinking.

He opened his door. "Look, why don't I ask Cleo if you can squeeze in with her and Jesse? That way if something happens—"

"Oh, right, then you'll be all alone," she snapped. "Good buddy system, Edan. Forget it, I'm coming too."

He gave her a long, measuring look, then grinned. "You got it, tiger. I'll be right back." He slipped out and head bent against the stinging snow, ran to the Jeep.

What am I doing? Natalie wondered, shivering as his door opened and he slid back inside.

"They're gonna let my parents know we'll be a couple miles behind them," he said, making a U-turn and creeping back onto the road. "Sit tight, Nat. We'll be up and back in no time."

"No time" stretched into overtime, which stretched Natalie's jangling nerves into near-panic. The closer to the cabin they got, the harder the snow fell and three

216

times they almost skidded off the side of the narrow, one lane road.

"There isn't even room to turn around, is there?" Natalie asked, gritting her teeth as the van lost traction.

"Nope," Edan said. His knuckles were white and his shoulders tense. "The only way out is up."

A gust of wind rocked the van and the tires spun free.

"We're in the blizzard, aren't we?" Natalie said, mashing her face against the window to try and spot their tire tracks but it was no use. The blinding snow covered them as soon as they were made.

"Yeah," Edan said, easing the van toward the cabin. The van strained, lost it and skidded into a massive snowdrift.

"Holy God," Natalie whispered. The walls of Fort Courage, built nearly three feet high, had merged with the surrounding landscape and the only thing visible was the streaming, red banner. "We're stuck here, aren't we Edan?"

"Yeah," he said wearily, tilting his head back against the seat and closing his eyes. His face was pale and strained. "Sorry, Nat. We're gonna have to stay and wait it out." He glanced over at her and managed a crooked smile. "At least we have food, huh?"

And a fireplace and a dozen thick, cozy down comforters, she thought, shivering. She'd be dead when she got home, that was a given, but now her heart was racing and every inch of her body was wired with anticipation. She glanced down at her knotted fingers, avoiding his eyes and said demurely, "Why don't we go in then, before the storm gets even worse?"

Eighteen

"Kick back, Scarlett, we've got a long haul ahead," Simon said, grinning across the Bronco at Maria, who was trying to find a comfortable position. "Here." He eased back into the corner, shifting so he was at an angle. "Lean against me and you can stretch your legs out across the seat."

Maria gave him a speculative look. He was doing it again, getting physical in a calm, sort of experimental way that pushed the boundaries of friendship into new and unexplored territory. He probably considers himself some kind of pioneer, she thought suddenly, smirking. He was so bizarre but wasn't that what she liked about him? The fact that he viewed life as one vast, unscripted Oprah show and would veer off in whatever direction the panelist of the moment needed to go?

"What's with the Cheshire Cat grin?" he said.

"You don't look very comfortable," she said, running her gaze over his long, lean body and thinking what a lie that was. He looked *too* comfortable.

"I'm like water," he drawled. "I adapt to the shape of the container. Go ahead, give it a belly flop, you'll see."

"You are so weird," she said, leaning back against him. Her body curved into his, her head cradled perfectly into the hollow between his shoulder and neck. Her arms, searching for a resting place, found one along his bent leg and the other traced his, which loosely encircled her waist.

"So?" he murmured. "How's the water, Scarlett?"

"Sauna-city," she said, shivering.

"Hey," Janis said, craning her neck over the seat and giving them a startled look. "Are you guys going out or something?"

"Nah," Simon said lightly, smiling down at Maria. "We're just friends."

"Do you think they're really just friends?" Janis whispered to Brian, trying her hardest not to look into the backseat. She couldn't believe they were all twined together like wisteria vines, laughing and looking totally into each other. "I wonder what the real deal is."

"Why don't you just butt out?" Brian asked, braking slightly as Joey's brakelights flared. "I mean, the last time you got involved with Maria's life, look what happened."

"Hey." Janis was hurt. "Coach Garry worked out fine."

He snorted. "By your standards."

"Don't tell me you're still sulking because he's leaving at the end of the year?" she said, staring at him. "C'mon Brian, who cares if he was a good coach? He was a hound."

"Look, just drop it, okay?"

"But I don't want to drop it—"

"Would you just do me one favor, one time, please?" he ground out. "Just forget about what *you* want for one minute and let me concentrate on getting us home alive? You think you can do that or will it violate some activist principle that says nobody else is allowed to have a want of their own?"

"You're really mean," Janis said, once she could speak.

"Yeah," he said grimly, squinting through the windshield. "Today I think I am."

"No wonder Jett bites you," she mumbled. "I'd bite you too if I wasn't afraid I'd catch something—"

"You just can't stop, can you?" he said.

"—like jock itch," she continued, too embarrassed and indignant to shut up. "Or maybe terminal, tight-enditis."

" 'Welcome to Chandler,' " Joey read, eyeing the sign on the outskirts of town. "Man, I never thought I'd be so happy to be home. Okay, kids, who gets dropped off first?"

"Faizon, I guess," Cassandra said, snuggling in his arms. She was cramping something wicked and even though she was thrilled she wasn't pregnant, she wasn't distracted enough to forget what would happen if her mother found out Faizon had gone skiing with them. She sighed. If only they could be together again, this time with birth control and with no need to keep their ears open for cars and keys jingling in the locks.

"Where to, Faizon?" Joey asked, eyeing him in the mirror.

"The men's shelter up by the highway," Faizon said, flushing slightly. "I rent a room there."

Joey's eyebrows rose. "Isn't that place a little dangerous?"

"I haven't had a problem," Faizon said, stroking Cassandra's hair and smiling down at her. "Other than not being able to bring Cassandra home with me, that is."

"So then where do you guys see each other?" Joey asked.

"No where, really," Cassandra said. "I mean, when I was in the hospital it was easy but now that I'm home, well . . ."

"It won't be like this forever," Faizon murmured, kissing her. "I'll be able to afford a place of my own someday."

Stephanie sat up front, listening to the conversation and wondering, with a spark of excitement, why she hadn't thought of this sooner. Probably because she'd never been in the position to *help* someone before. Her whole life had been structured around surviving instead of sharing.

"How much do you pay a month, Faizon?" she asked, swiveling in her seat. "I mean, I know that's a personal question . . ."

"No problem," he said easily, naming a figure.

Her pulses quickened. The figure he'd named was higher than what they'd been asking for rent. "Does that include meals?"

"Not food, just the use of the kitchen," he said and shot her a rueful smile. "And believe me, that kitchen's been *used*."

"Hey, Faizon," Stephanie said slowly, tucking her hair behind her ear. "If I could offer you a room in a private home for less money with the same use of the kitchen,

221

what would you say?" She glanced at Cassandra, whose wide, doe eyes were starting to glow.

"Sounds too good to be true," he said, grinning. "Who's the landlord, you?"

"Yeah," Stephanie said, meeting his startled gaze.

"For real?"

"Yeah," she said, laughing. "So . . . ?"

"I'll take it," he said and leaning forward, shook on it.

"Want me to make coffee?" Natalie said awkwardly. Edan had turned the water and the generator back on, built a roaring fire, retrieved several duffle bags from the van and now they were alone in the snug cabin. No TV, no radio, only the buffeting wind and crackling fire breaking the silence. Everywhere she looked there was a couch or a bed, something to remind her that darkness was falling and sooner or later, they would have to sleep.

"Yeah, let me just warm up for a second before I make the food run," he said, teeth chattering. He was standing in front of the fireplace, fumbling with his snow-caked gloves. "My hands are so numb I can't get these things off."

"Here, I'll do it," she said, crossing the room. She took his hands, shivering in spite of the roaring fire and tugged off the sodden gloves. "God, Edan, your hands are like ice," she said, rubbing them between her own. "Maybe we should forget about the food. I don't want to have to drag your butt back inside after you freeze into an icicle or anything." She made the mistake of glancing up and found him watching her with a soft, curious look.

222

"Hey, tiger," he said, putting his cold hand to her burning cheek. "Good to see you again."

Yes, she breathed silently as his mouth covered hers with a slow, piercing sweetness. Oh yeah, this is it, this is—

The front door flew open and a blast of frigid, snowy air whirled into the room. A frozen, snow-covered figure lurched in and with a feeble, croaked, "Help," collapsed on the floor.

"Get the door, Natalie," Edan said, whipping around the table and gently rolling the deathly still figure onto its back.

Natalie locked the door and came up alongside him, staring down at the pale, waxy face.

It was the girl with the fur mittens from the general store.

"Oh, great," Natalie said, completely disgusted.

Look for *Girl Friends #6: Daydream Believer* in your bookstore next month!